D1015447

JOHNNY BOO AND THE ICE CREAM COMPUTER

JAMES KOCHALKA

TOP SHELF PRODUCTIONS

A PHOTO OF THE AUTHOR:

Johnny Boo and the Ice Cream Computer © 2018 James Kochalka.

Published by Top Shelf Productions, PO Box 1282, Marietta, GA 30061-1282, USA. Top Shelf Productions is an imprint of IDW Publishing, a division of Idea and Design Works, LLC. Offices: 2765 Truxtun Road, San Diego, CA 92106. Top Shelf Productions®, the Top Shelf logo, Idea and Design Works®, and the IDW logo are registered trademarks of Idea and Design Works, LLC. All Rights Reserved. With the exception of small excerpts of artwork used for review purposes, none of the contents of this publication may be reprinted without the permission of IDW Publishing. IDW Publishing does not read or accept unsolicited submissions of ideas, stories, or artwork.

Editor-in-Chief: Chris Staros.

Edited by Leigh Walton.

Visit our online catalog at www.topshelfcomix.com.

Printed in Korea.

ISBN 978-1-60309-435-1

22   21   20   19   5   4   3   2

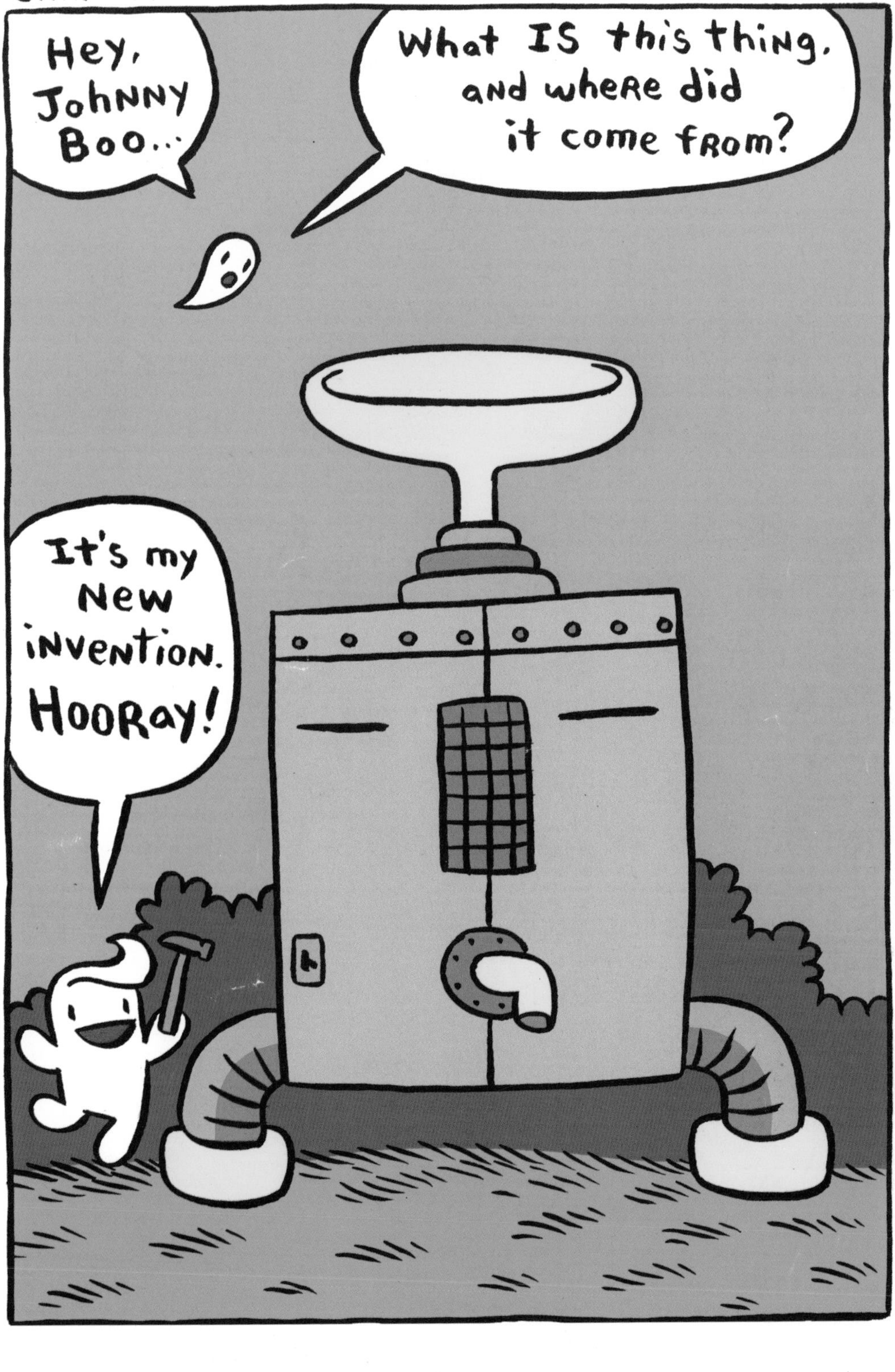
Hey, Johnny Boo...
What IS this thing, and where did it come from?
It's my new invention. Hooray!

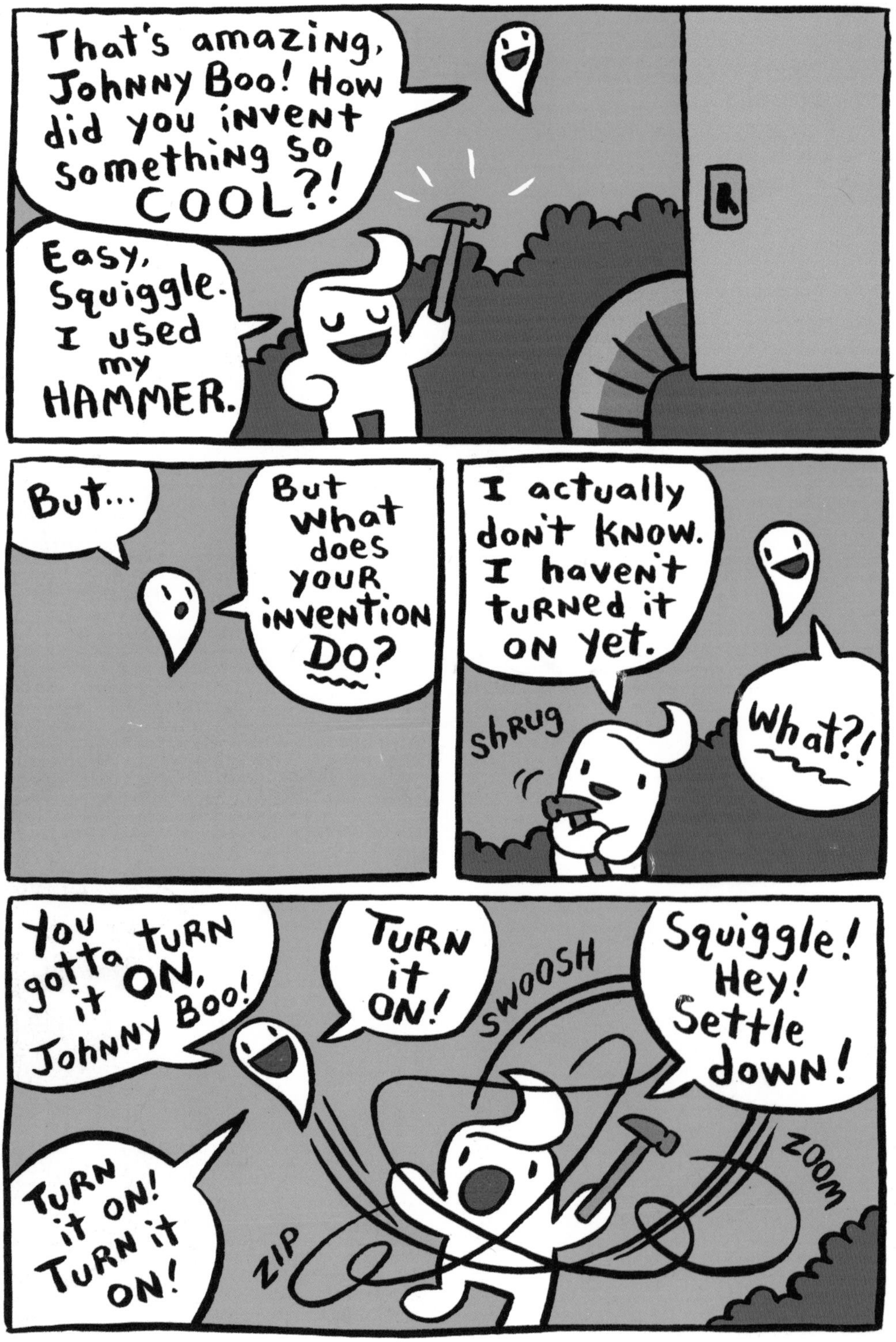

That's amazing, Johnny Boo! How did you invent something so COOL?!
Easy, Squiggle. I used my HAMMER.
But...
But what does your invention DO?
I actually don't know. I haven't turned it on yet.
SHRUG
What?!
You gotta turn it ON, Johnny Boo!
TURN it ON!
SWOOSH
Squiggle! Hey! Settle down!
TURN it ON! TURN it ON!
ZIP
ZOOM

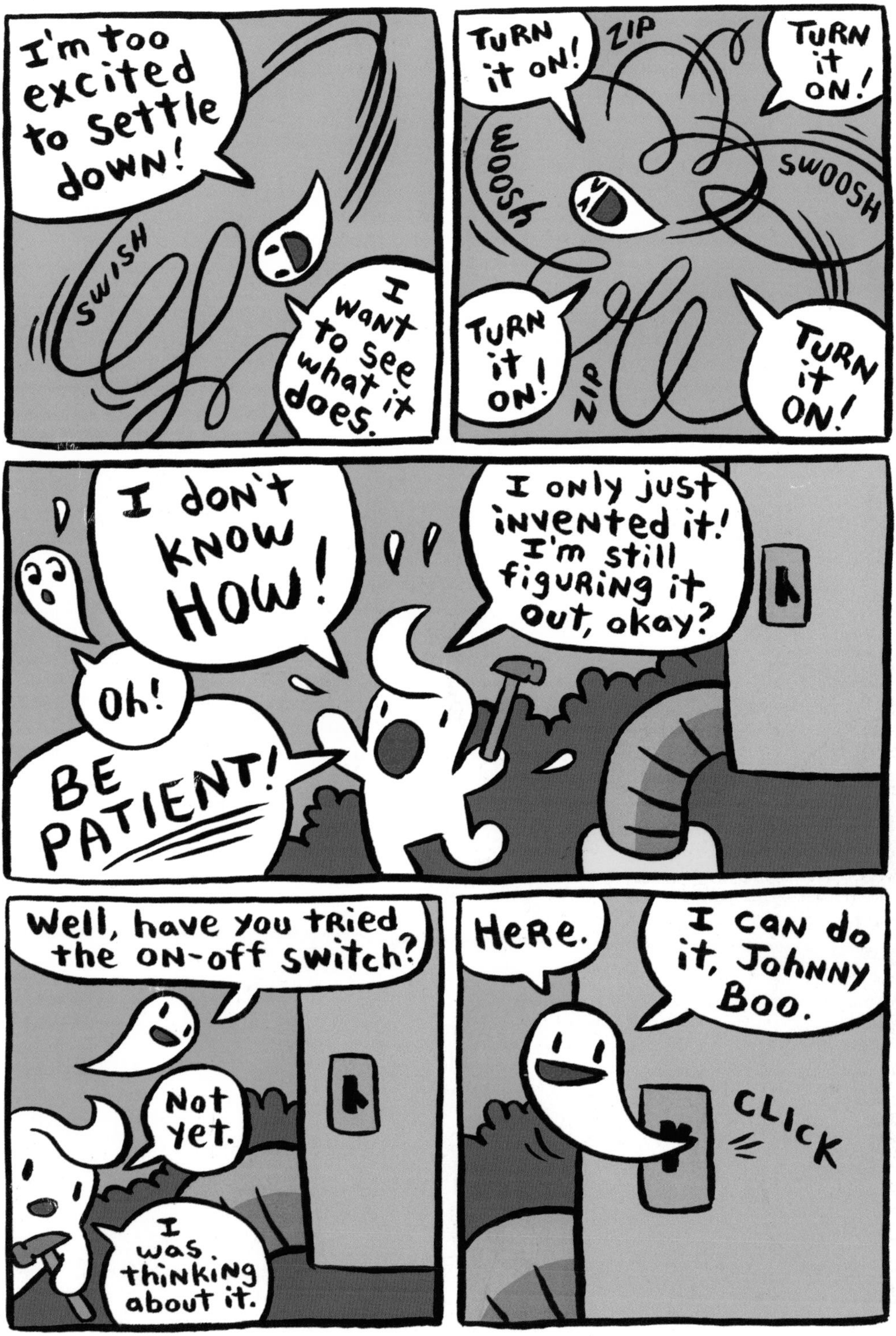
I'm too excited to settle down!
SWISH
I want to see what it does.
TURN it ON!
ZIP
TURN it ON!
WOOSH
SWOOSH
TURN it ON!
ZIP
TURN it ON!
I don't KNOW HOW!
I only just invented it! I'm still figuring it out, okay?
Oh!
BE PATIENT!
Well, have you tried the ON-off switch?
Not yet.
I was thinking about it.
Here.
I can do it, Johnny Boo.
CLICK

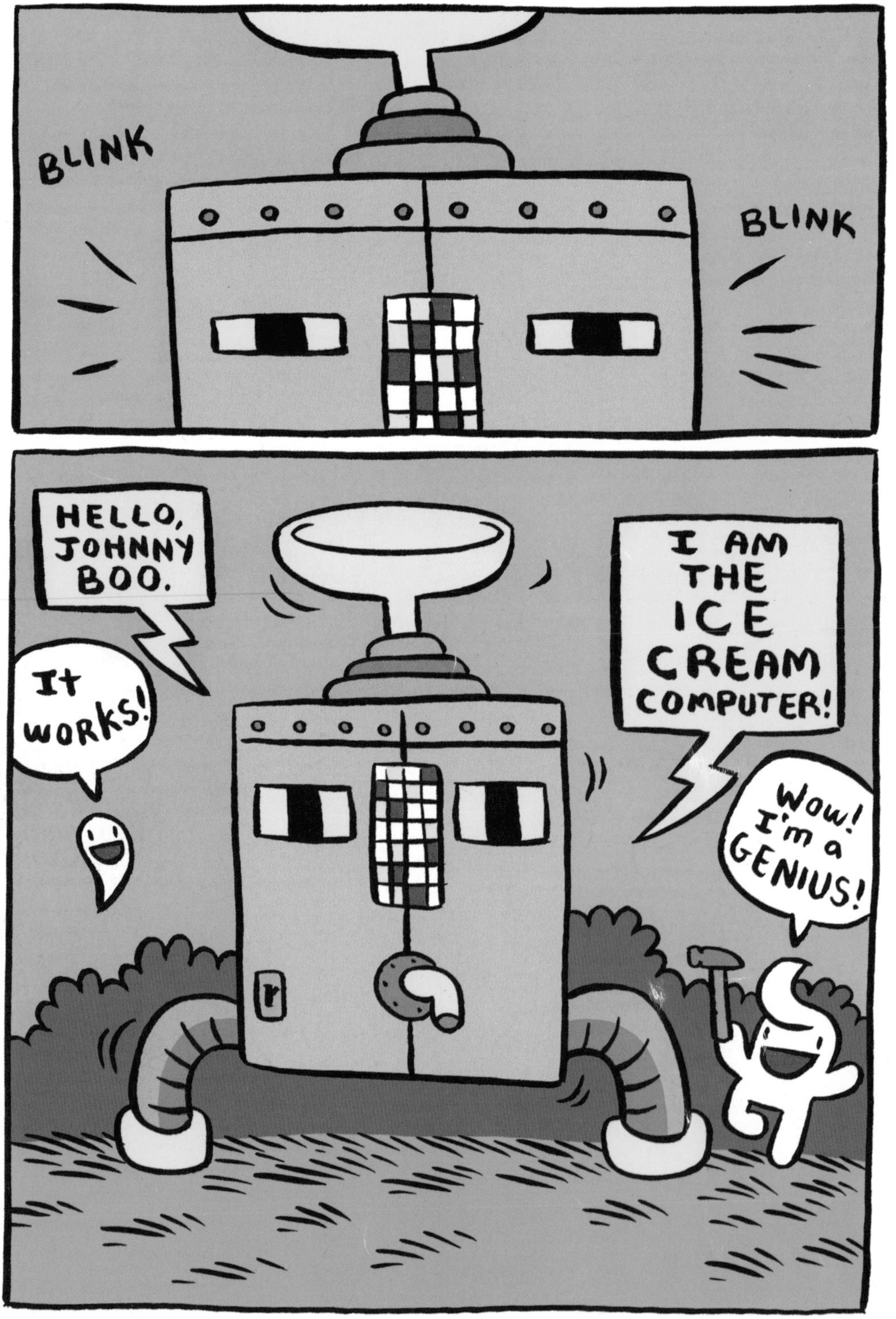
BLINK
BLINK
HELLO, JOHNNY BOO.
It works!
I AM THE ICE CREAM COMPUTER!
Wow! I'm a GENIUS!

CHAPTER TWO

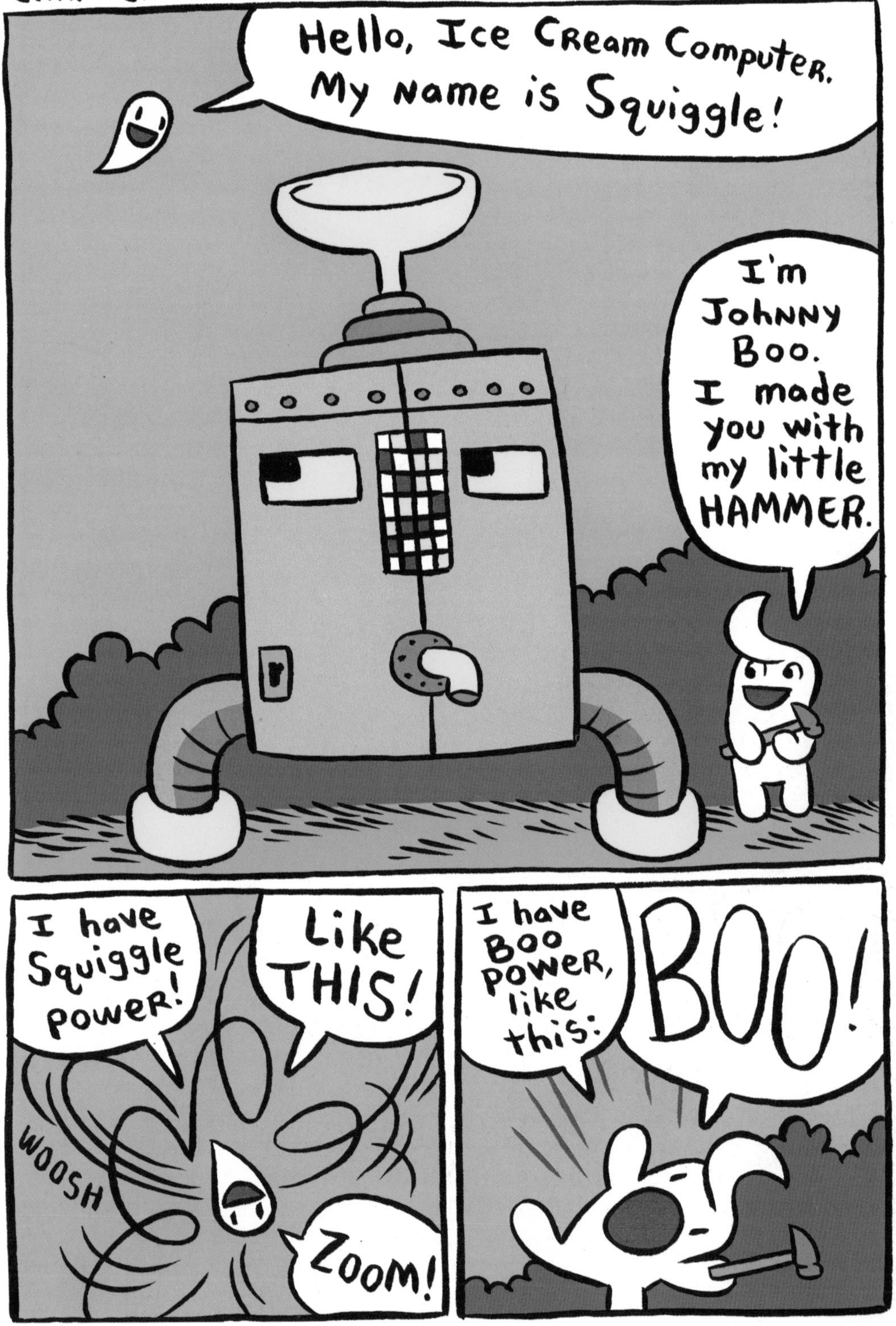
Hello, Ice Cream Computer. My name is Squiggle!
I'm Johnny Boo. I made you with my little HAMMER.
I have Squiggle power!
Like THIS!
WOOSH
ZOOM!
I have Boo power, like this:
BOO!

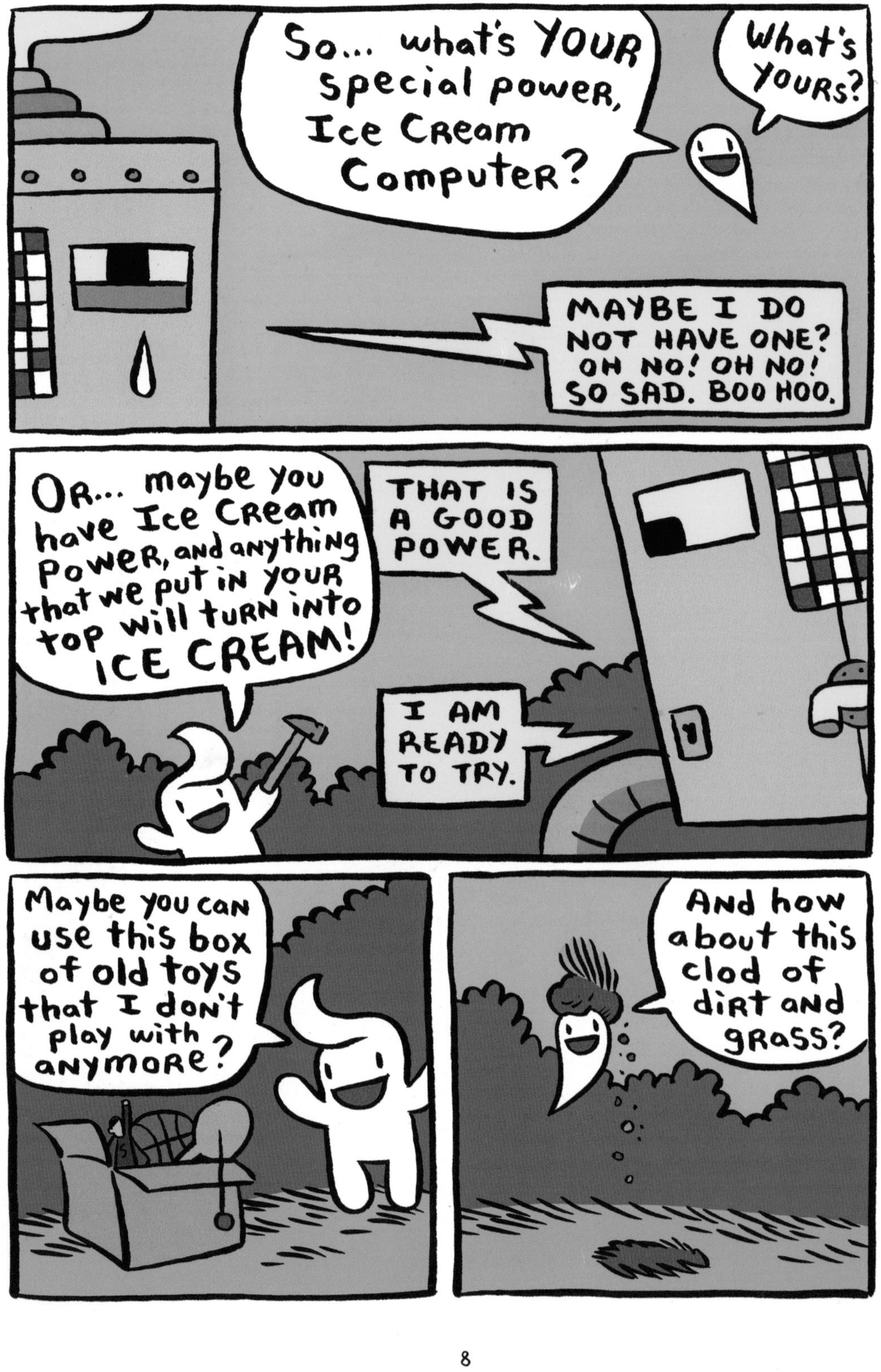
So... what's YOUR special power, Ice Cream Computer?
What's yours?
MAYBE I DO NOT HAVE ONE? OH NO! OH NO! SO SAD. BOO HOO.
OR... maybe you have Ice Cream Power, and anything that we put in your top will turn into ICE CREAM!
THAT IS A GOOD POWER.
I AM READY TO TRY.
Maybe you can use this box of old toys that I don't play with anymore?
And how about this clod of dirt and grass?

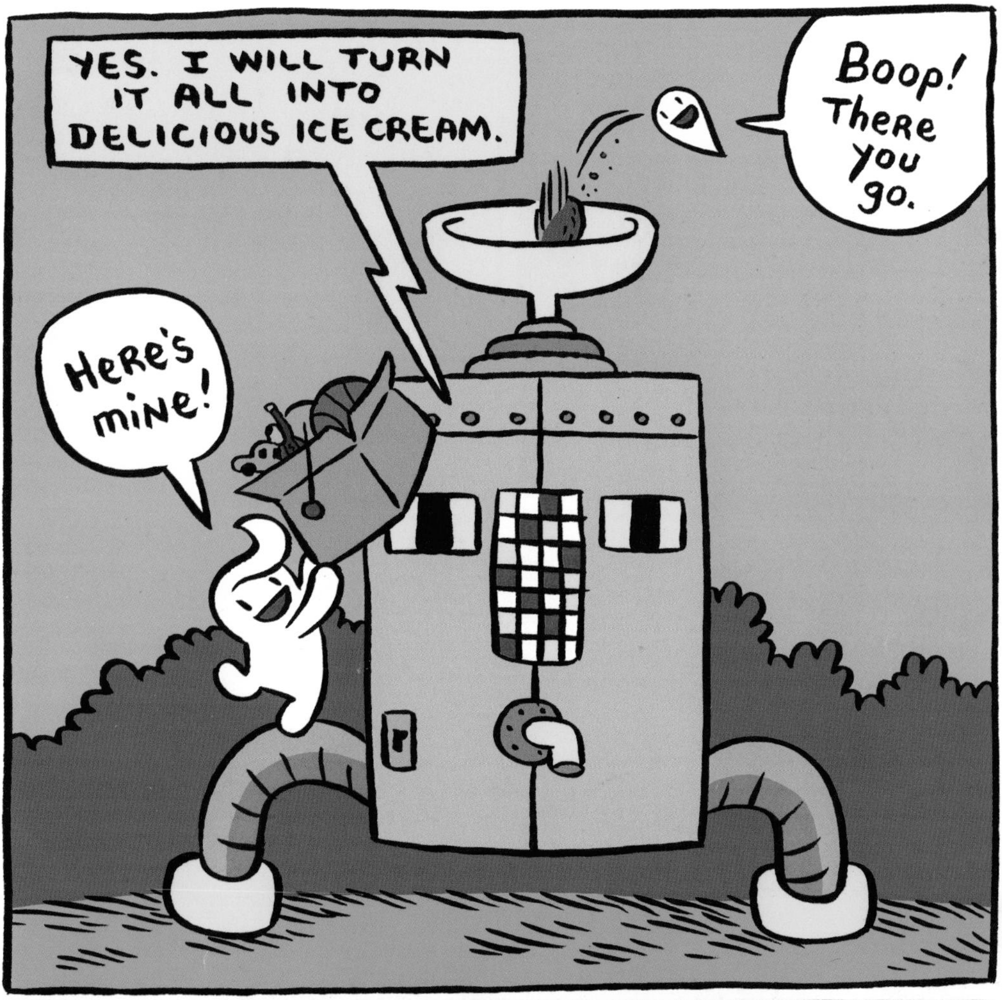
YES. I WILL TURN IT ALL INTO DELICIOUS ICE CREAM.
Boop! There you go.
Here's mine!

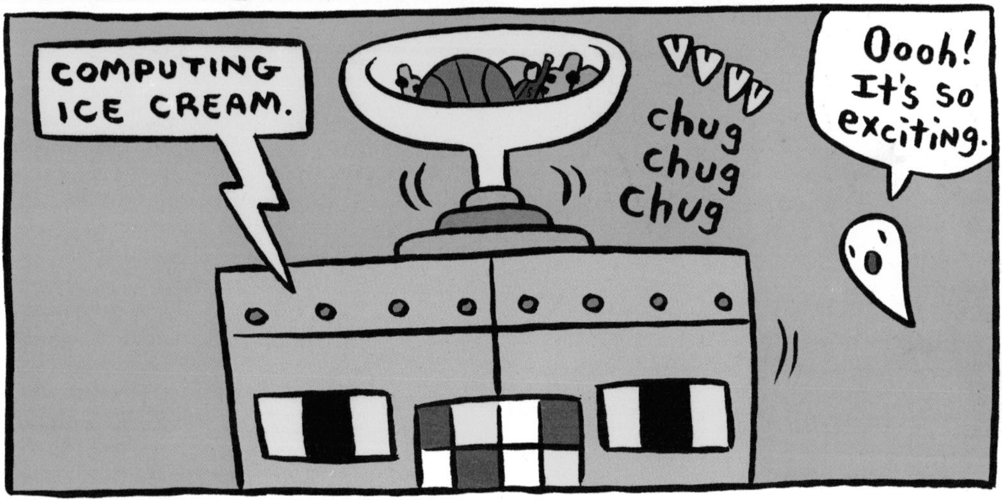
COMPUTING ICE CREAM.
chug chug chug
Oooh! It's so exciting.

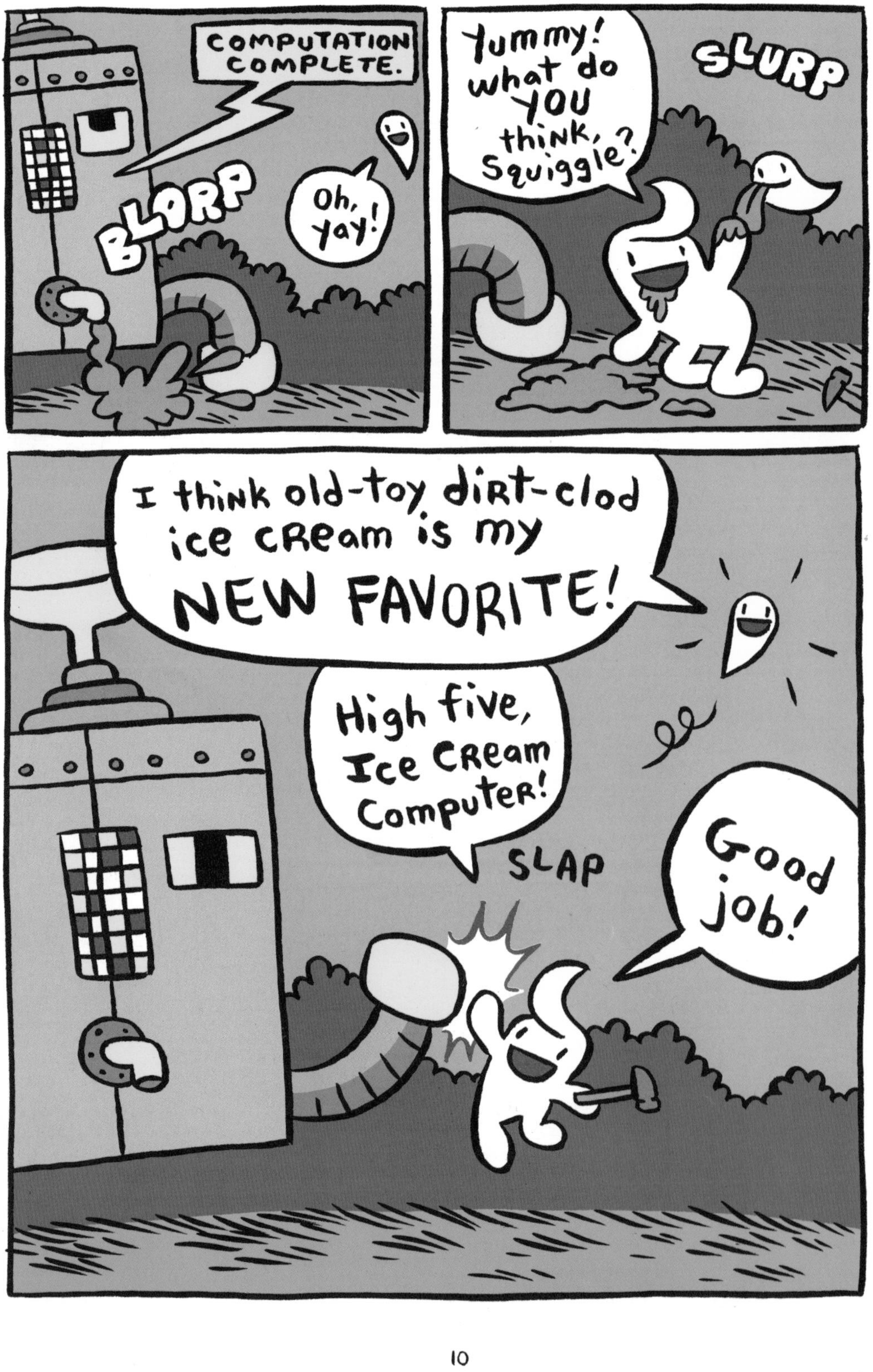
COMPUTATION COMPLETE.
BLORP
Oh, yay!
Yummy! what do YOU think, Squiggle?
SLURP
I think old-toy dirt-clod ice cream is my NEW FAVORITE!
High five, Ice Cream Computer!
SLAP
Good job!

CHAPTER THREE

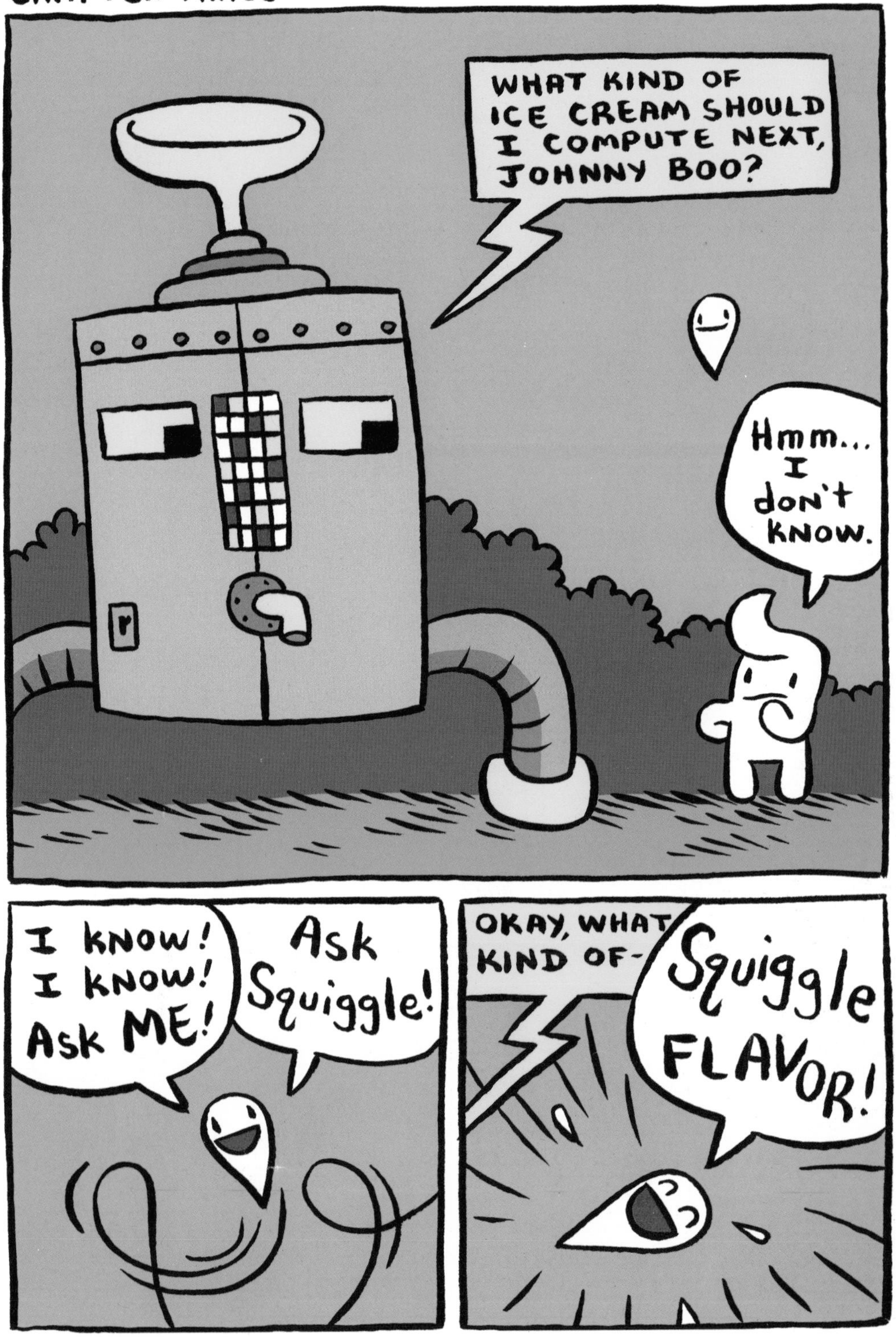
WHAT KIND OF ICE CREAM SHOULD I COMPUTE NEXT, JOHNNY BOO?
Hmm... I don't know.
I KNOW! I KNOW! ASK ME!
Ask Squiggle!
OKAY, WHAT KIND OF-
Squiggle FLAVOR!

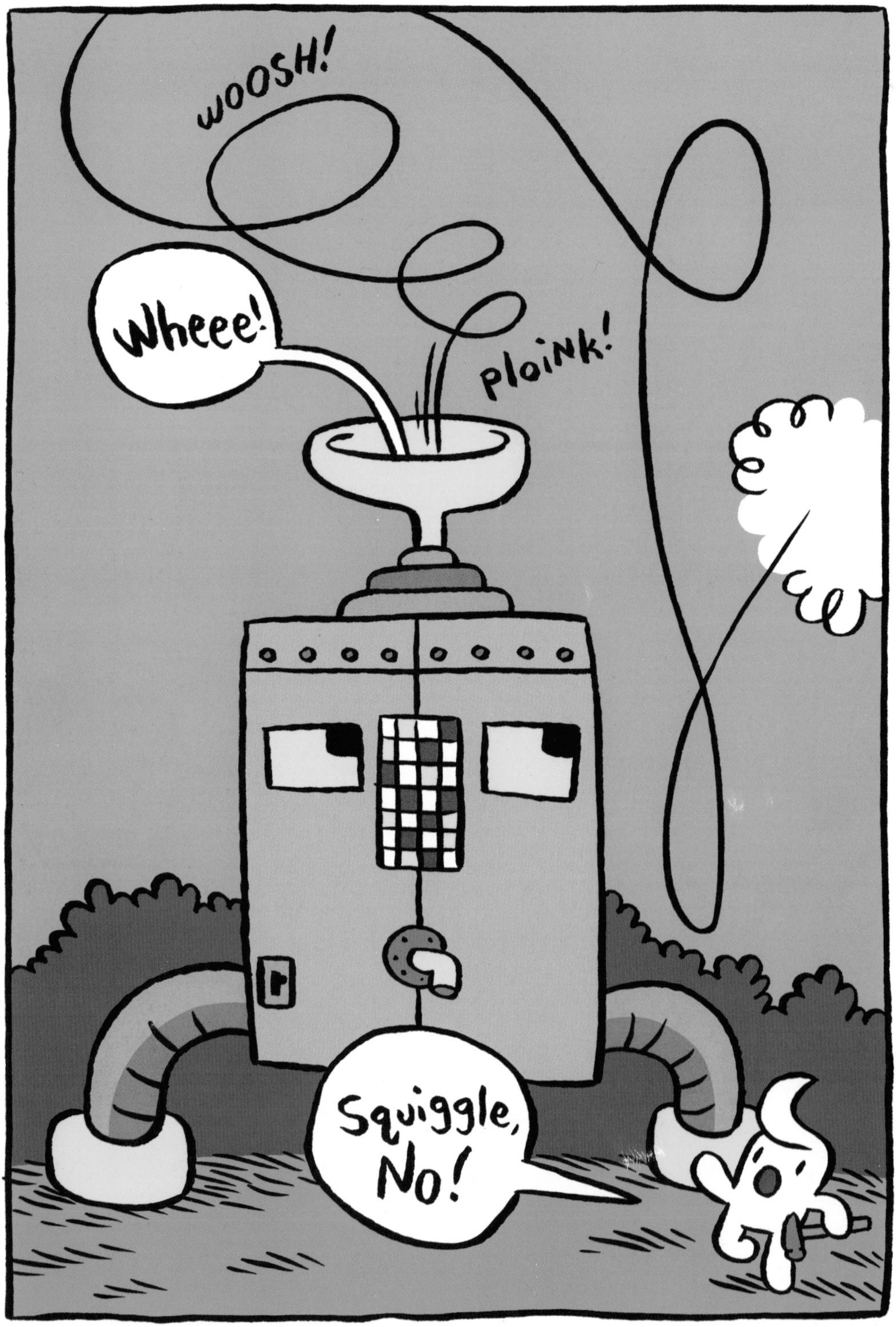
WOOSH!
Wheee!
PLOINK!
Squiggle, No!

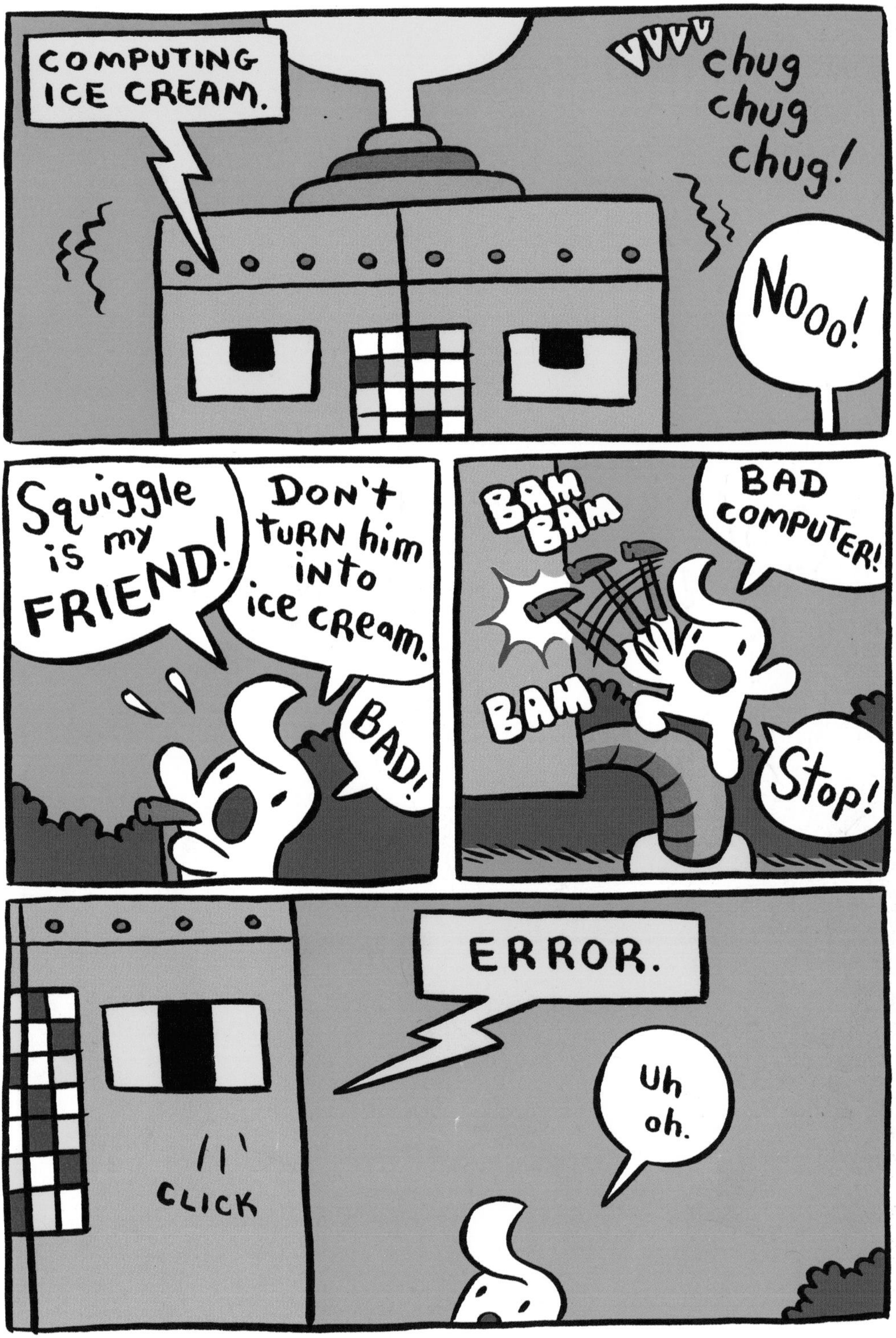
COMPUTING ICE CREAM.
VVVV chug chug chug!
Nooo!
Squiggle is my FRIEND!
Don't turn him into ice cream.
BAD!
BAM BAM
BAD COMPUTER!
BAM
Stop!
ERROR.
CLICK
Uh oh.

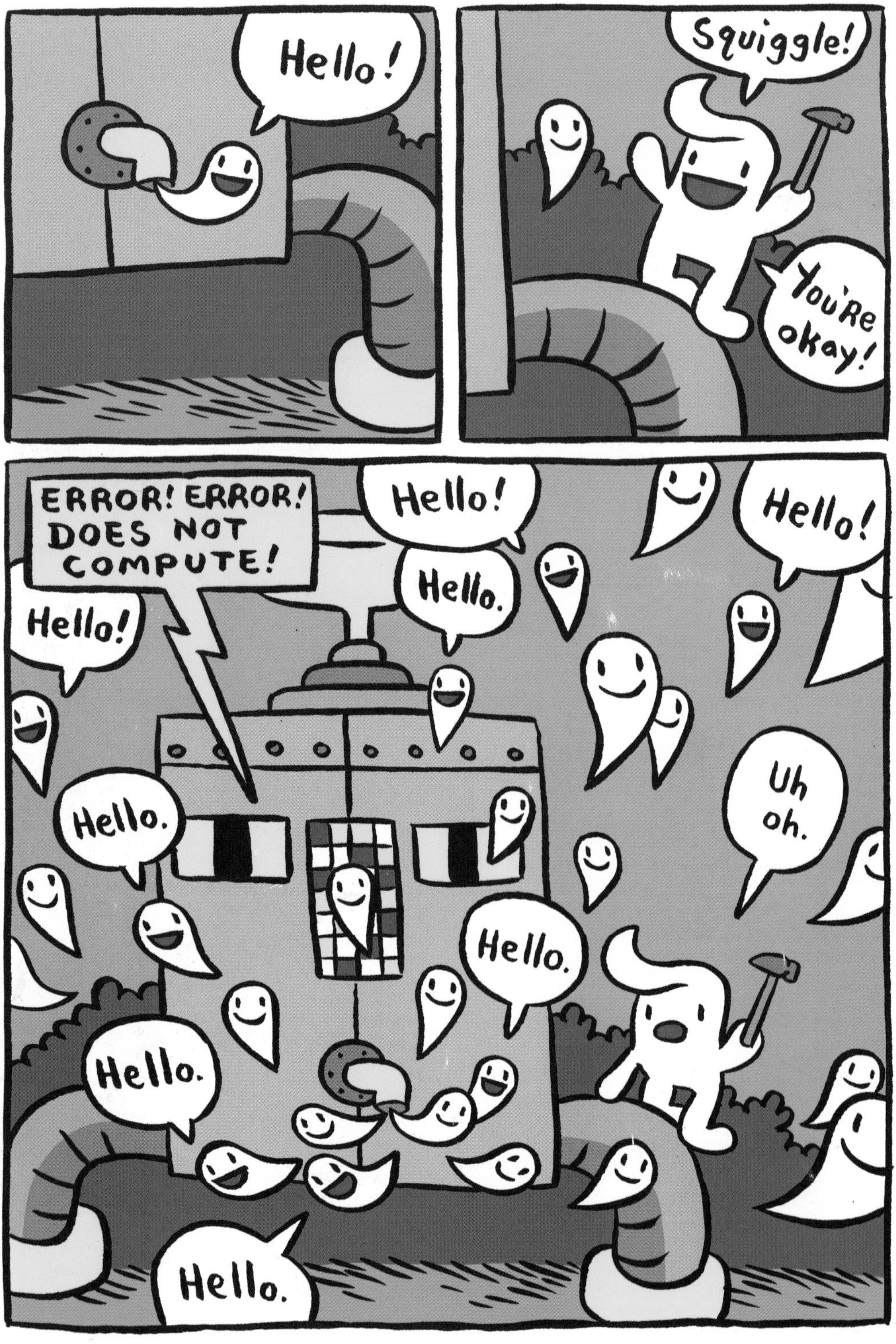
Hello!
Squiggle!
You're okay!
ERROR! ERROR! DOES NOT COMPUTE!
Hello!
Hello!
Hello.
Hello!
Hello.
Uh oh.
Hello.
Hello.
Hello.

CHAPTER FOUR

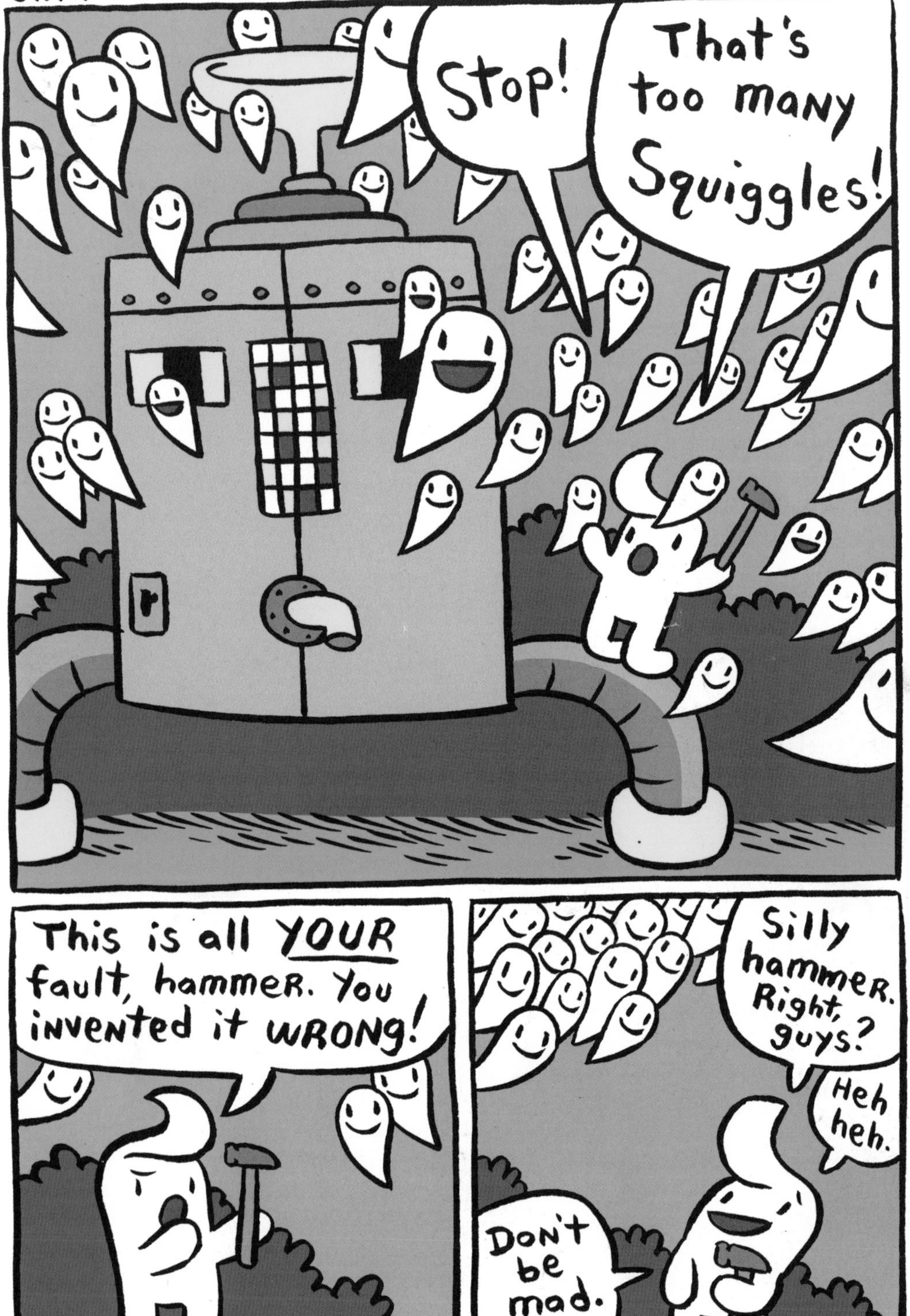
Stop!
That's too many Squiggles!
This is all YOUR fault, hammer. You invented it WRONG!
Silly hammer. Right, guys?
Heh heh.
Don't be mad.

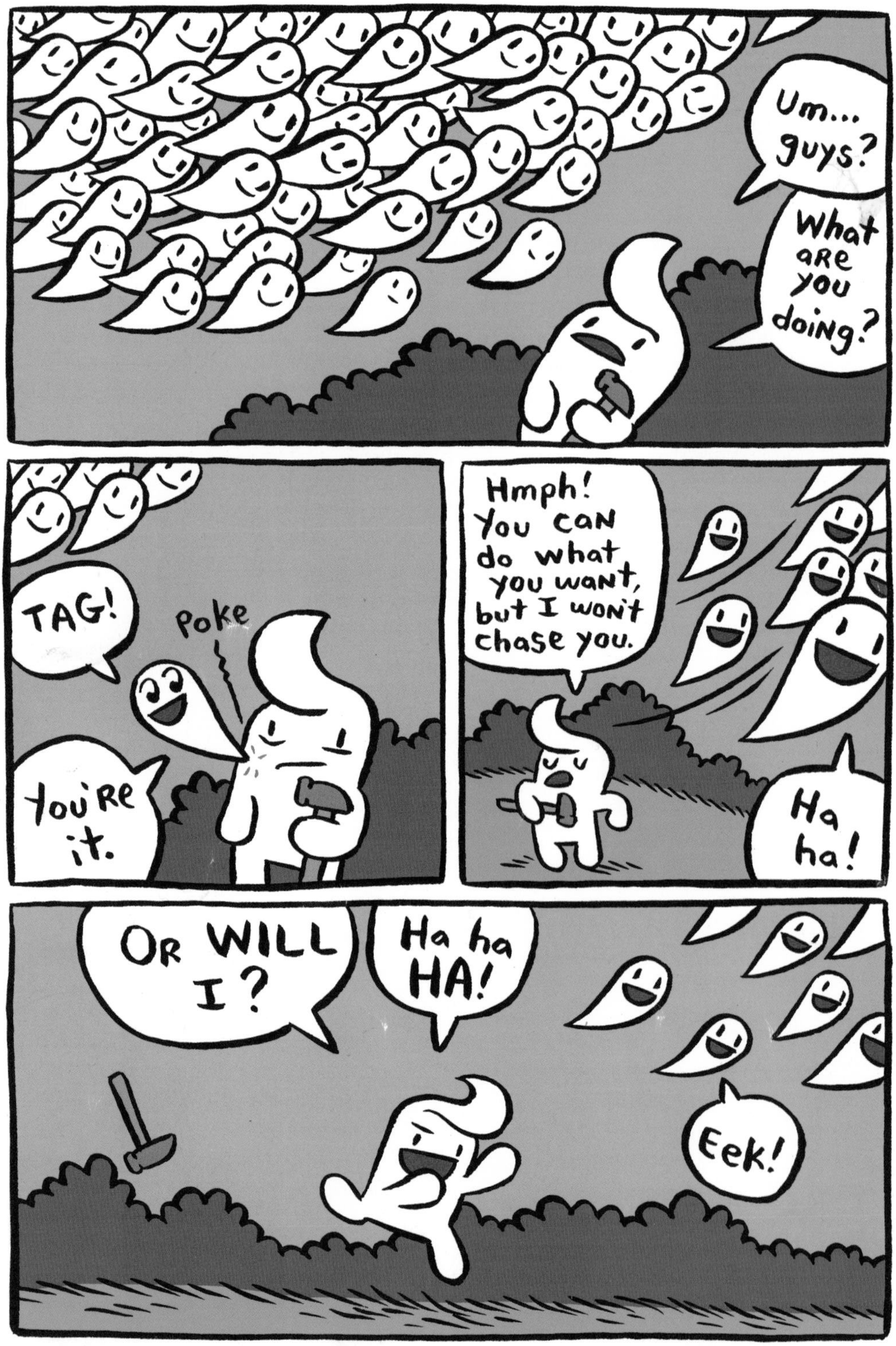

Um... guys?
What are you doing?
TAG!
Poke
You're it.
Hmph! You can do what you want, but I won't chase you.
Ha ha!
OR WILL I?
Ha ha HA!
Eek!

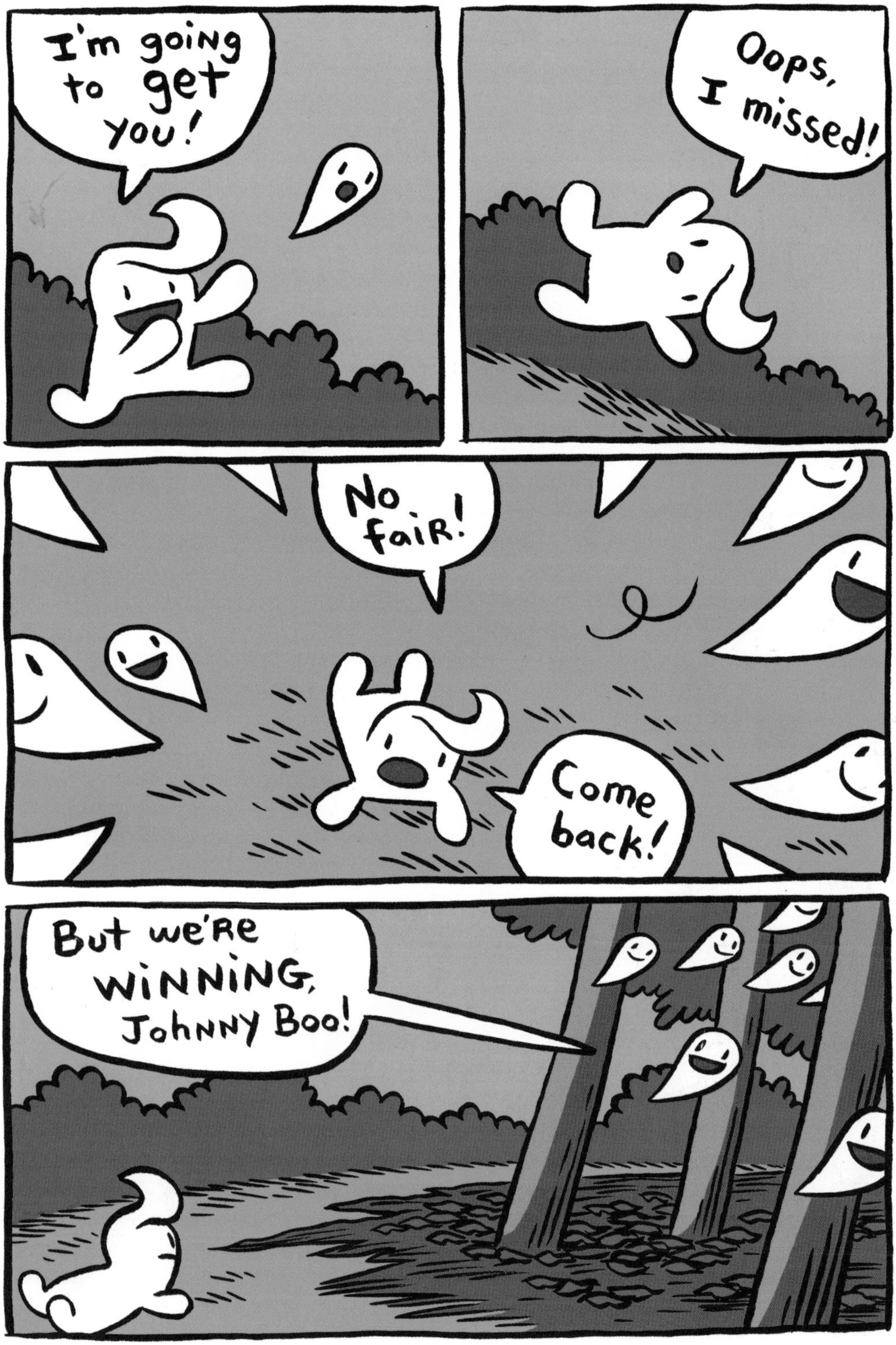
I'm going to get you!
Oops, I missed!
No fair!
Come back!
But we're WINNING, Johnny Boo!

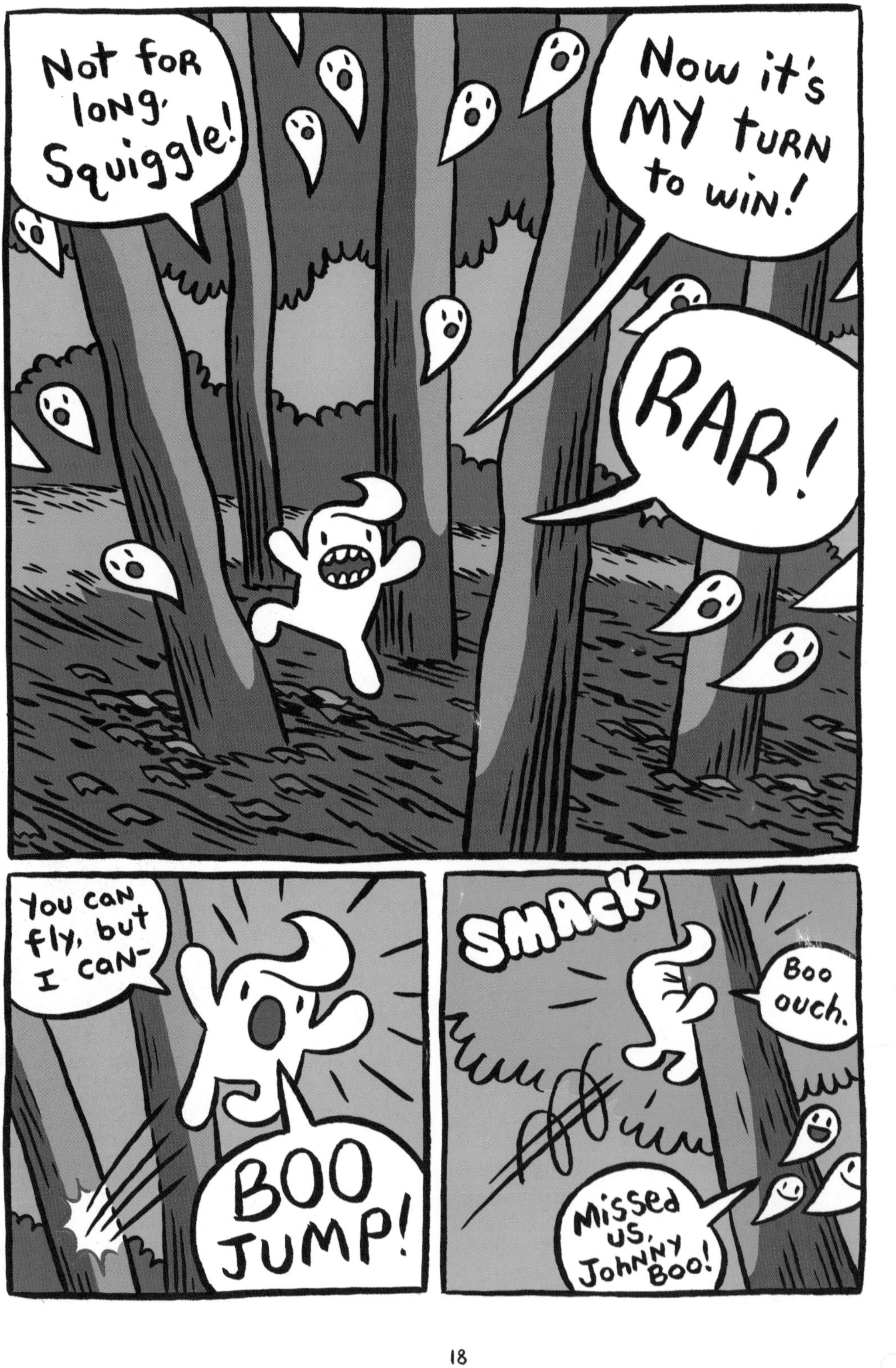

Not for long, Squiggle!
Now it's MY turn to win!
RAR!
You can fly, but I can-
BOO JUMP!
SMACK
Boo ouch.
Missed us, Johnny Boo!

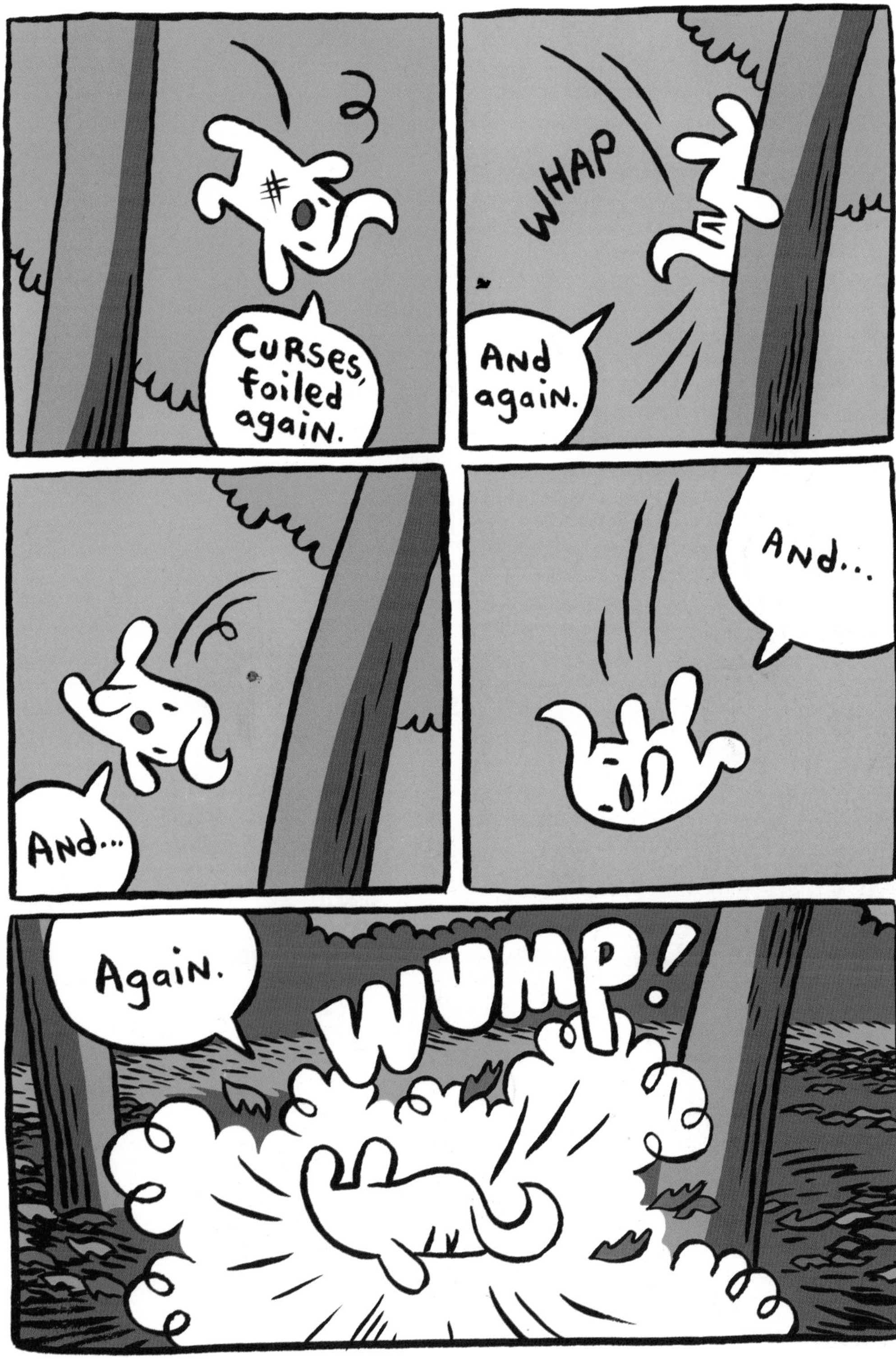
Curses, foiled again.
WHAP
And again.
And...
And...
Again.
WUMP!

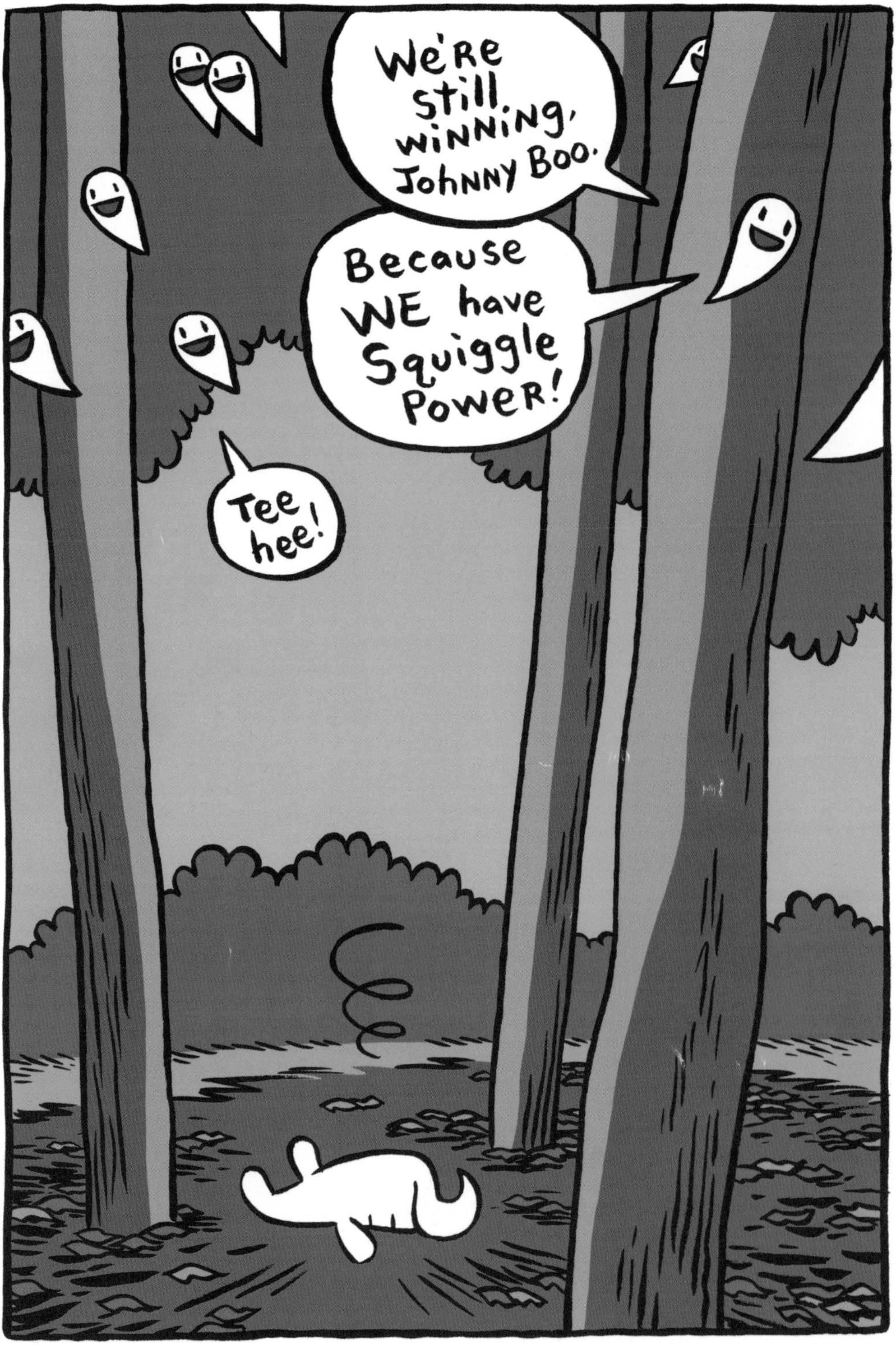
We're still winning, Johnny Boo.
Because WE have Squiggle Power!
Tee hee!

CHAPTER FIVE

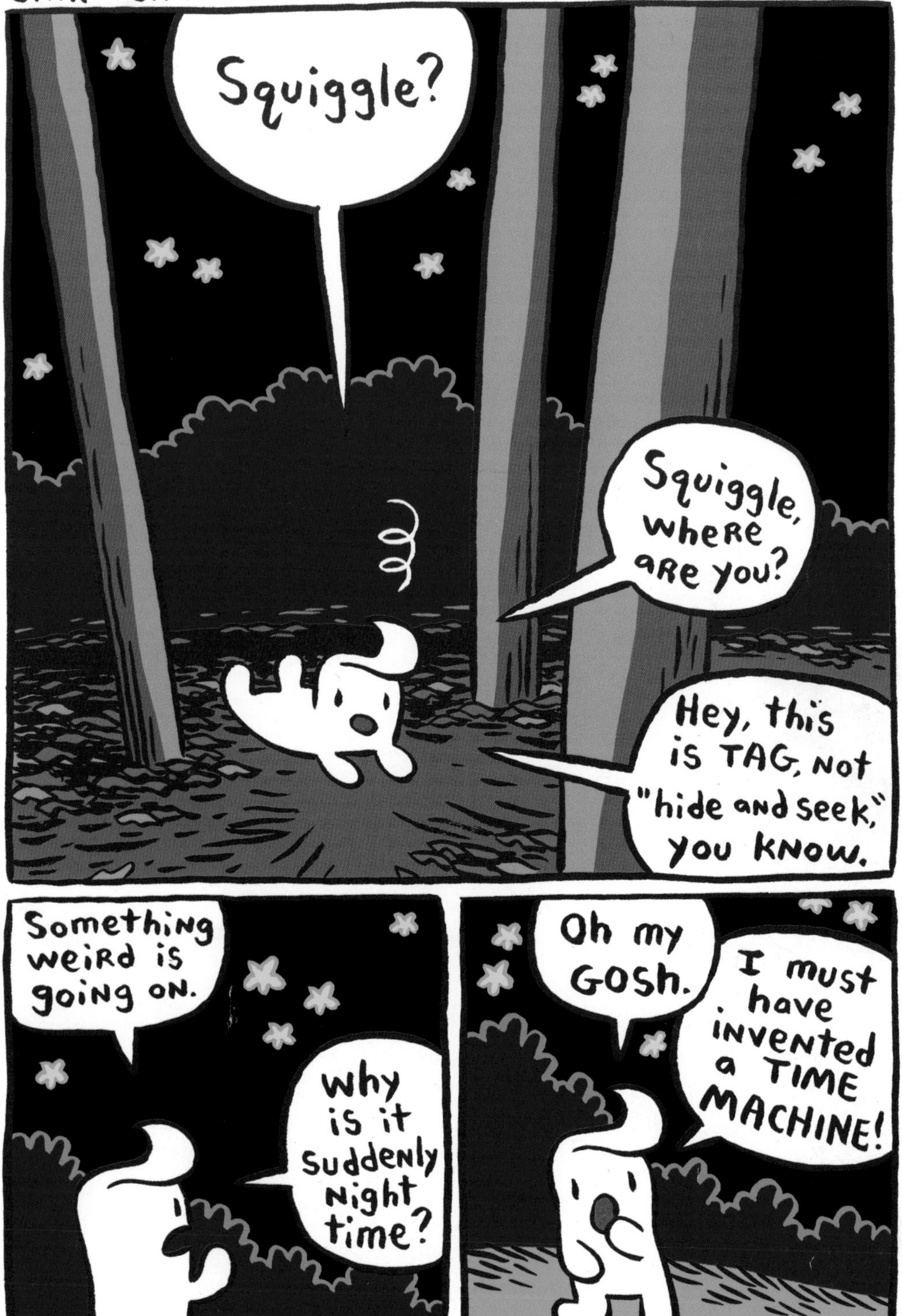
Squiggle?
Squiggle, where are you?
Hey, this is TAG, not "hide and seek," you know.
Something weird is going on.
Why is it suddenly Night time?
Oh my GOSh.
I must have invented a TIME MACHINE!

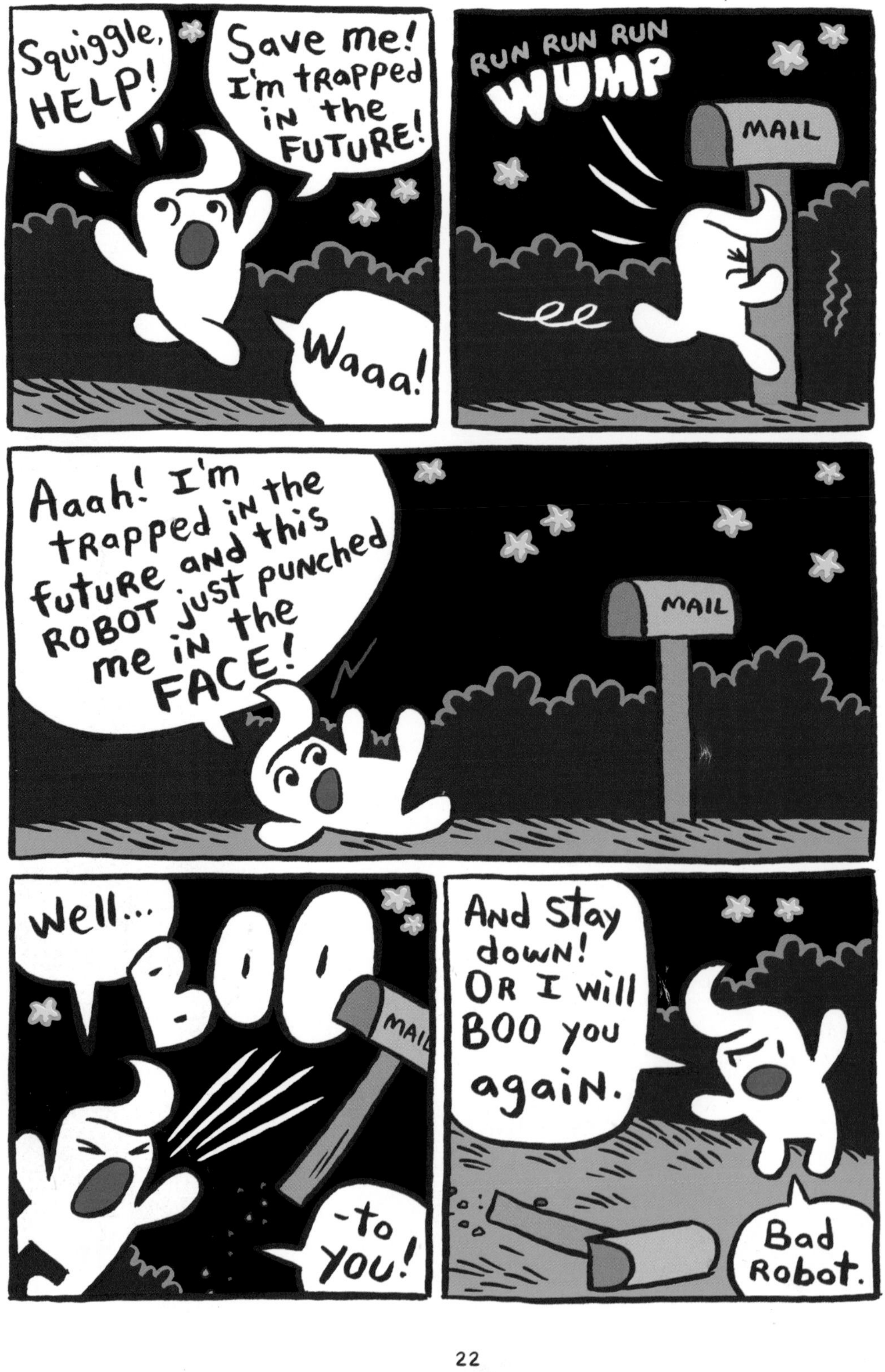
Squiggle, HELP!
Save me! I'm trapped in the FUTURE!
Waaa!
RUN RUN RUN
WUMP
MAIL
Aaah! I'm trapped in the future and this ROBOT just punched me in the FACE!
MAIL
Well...
BOO
-to you!
MAIL
And Stay down! OR I will BOO you again.
Bad Robot.

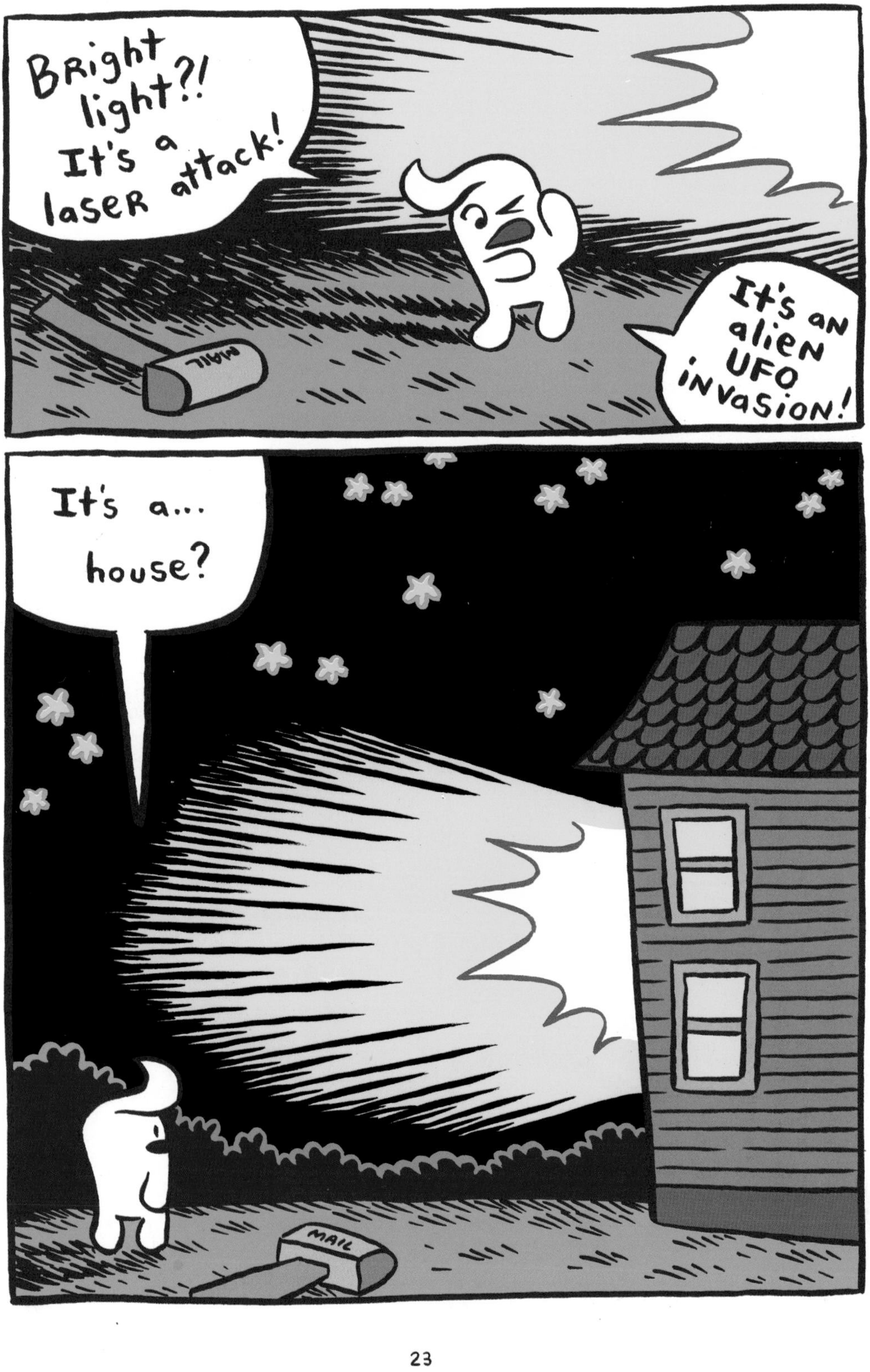
Bright light?! It's a laser attack!
It's an alien UFO invasion!
It's a... house?
MAIL

CHAPTER SIX

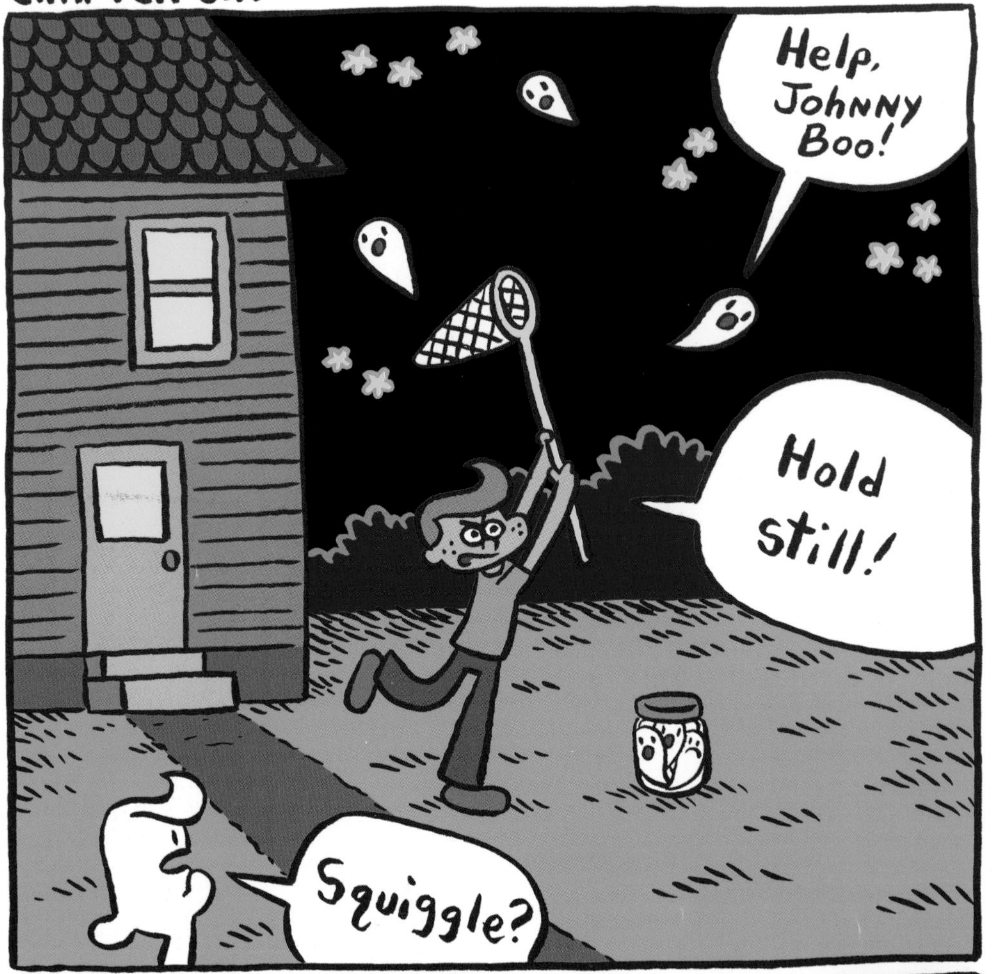
Help, Johnny Boo!
Hold still!
Squiggle?

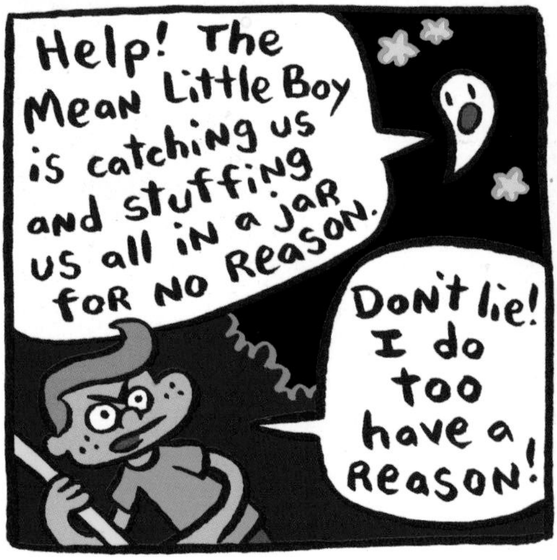
Help! The Mean Little Boy is catching us and stuffing us all in a jar for no reason.
Don't lie! I do too have a reason!

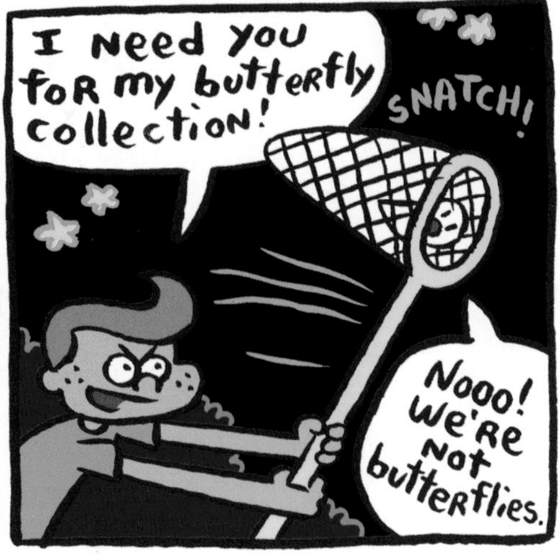
I need you for my butterfly collection!
SNATCH!
Nooo! We're not butterflies.

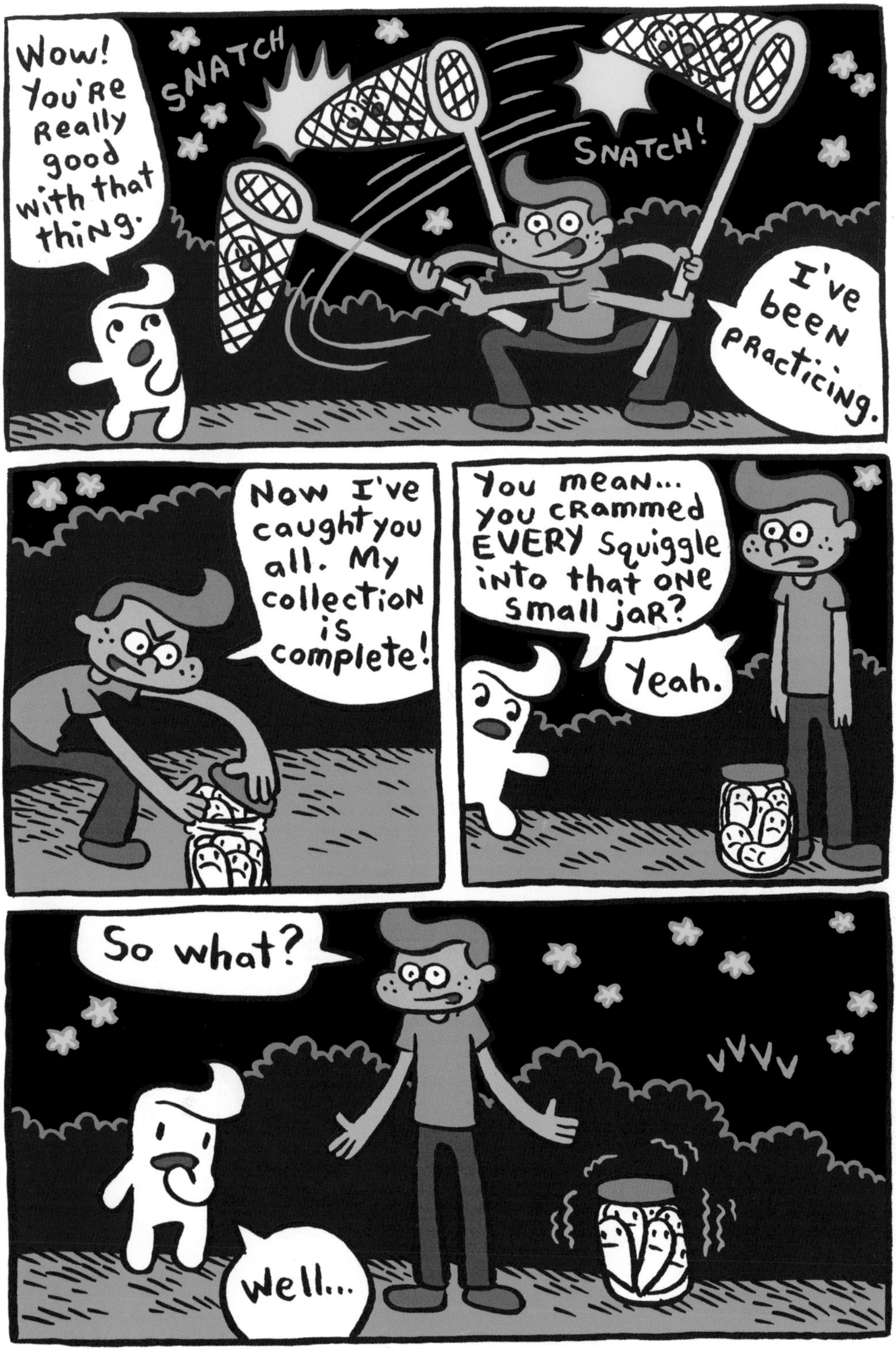

Wow! You're Really good with that thing.
SNATCH
SNATCH!
I've been practicing.
Now I've caught you all. My collection is complete!
You mean... you crammed EVERY Squiggle into that one small jar?
Yeah.
So what?
VVVV
Well...

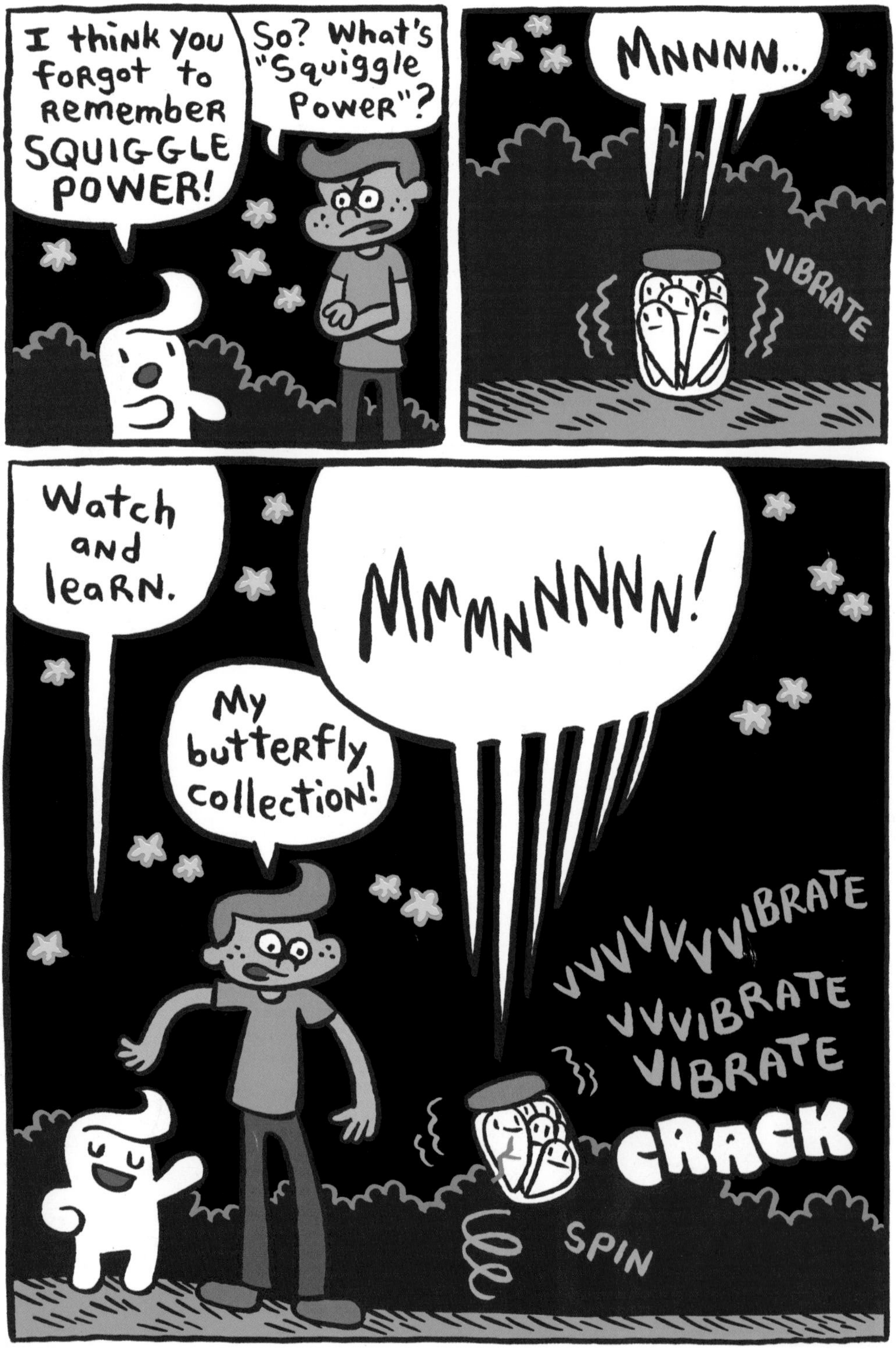
I think you forgot to remember SQUIGGLE POWER!
So? What's "Squiggle Power"?
MNNNN...
VIBRATE
Watch and learn.
MMMNNNNN!
My butterfly collection!
VVVVVVVVIBRATE
VVVIBRATE
VIBRATE
CRACK
SPIN

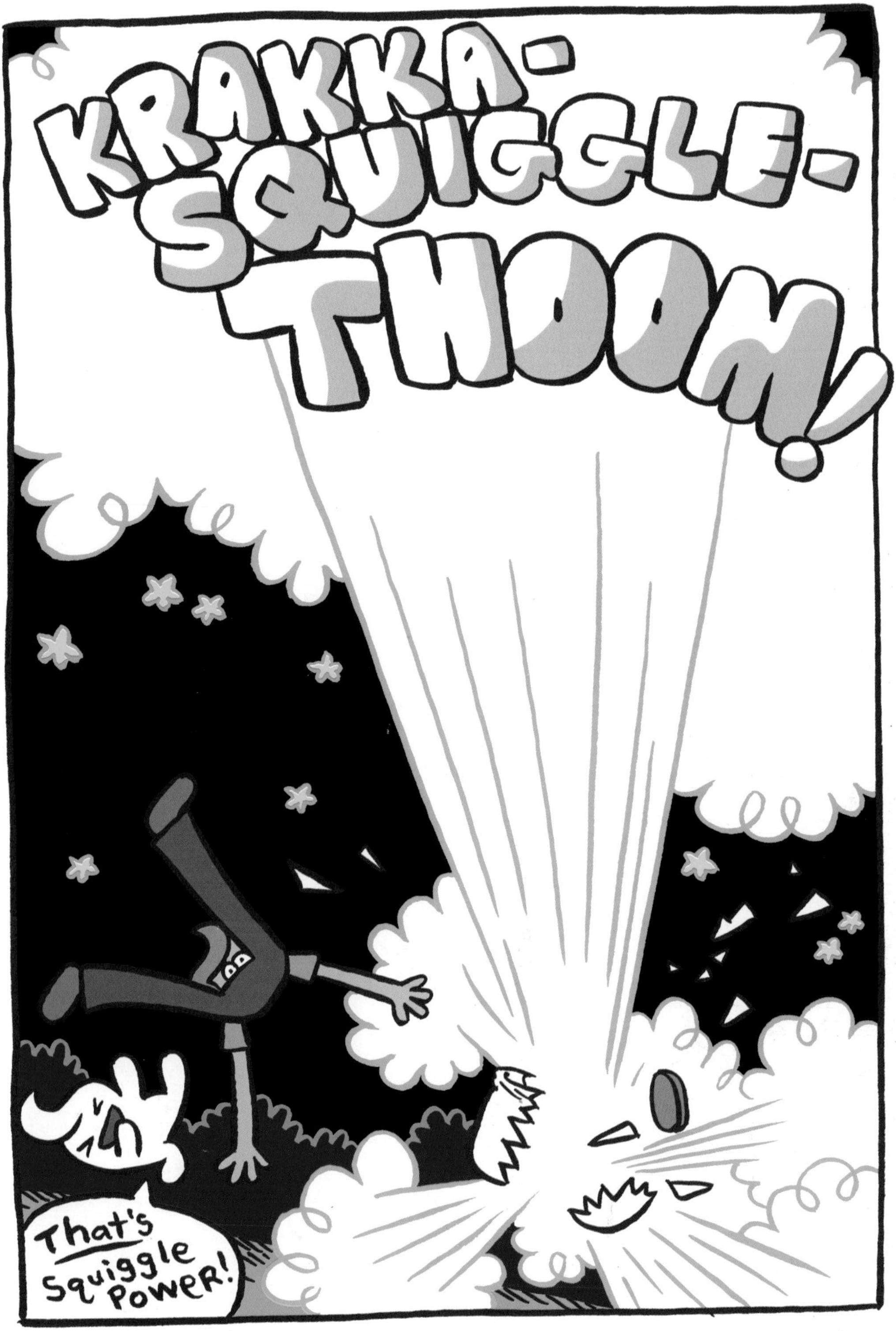
KRAKKA-SQUIGGLE-THOOM!
That's Squiggle Power!

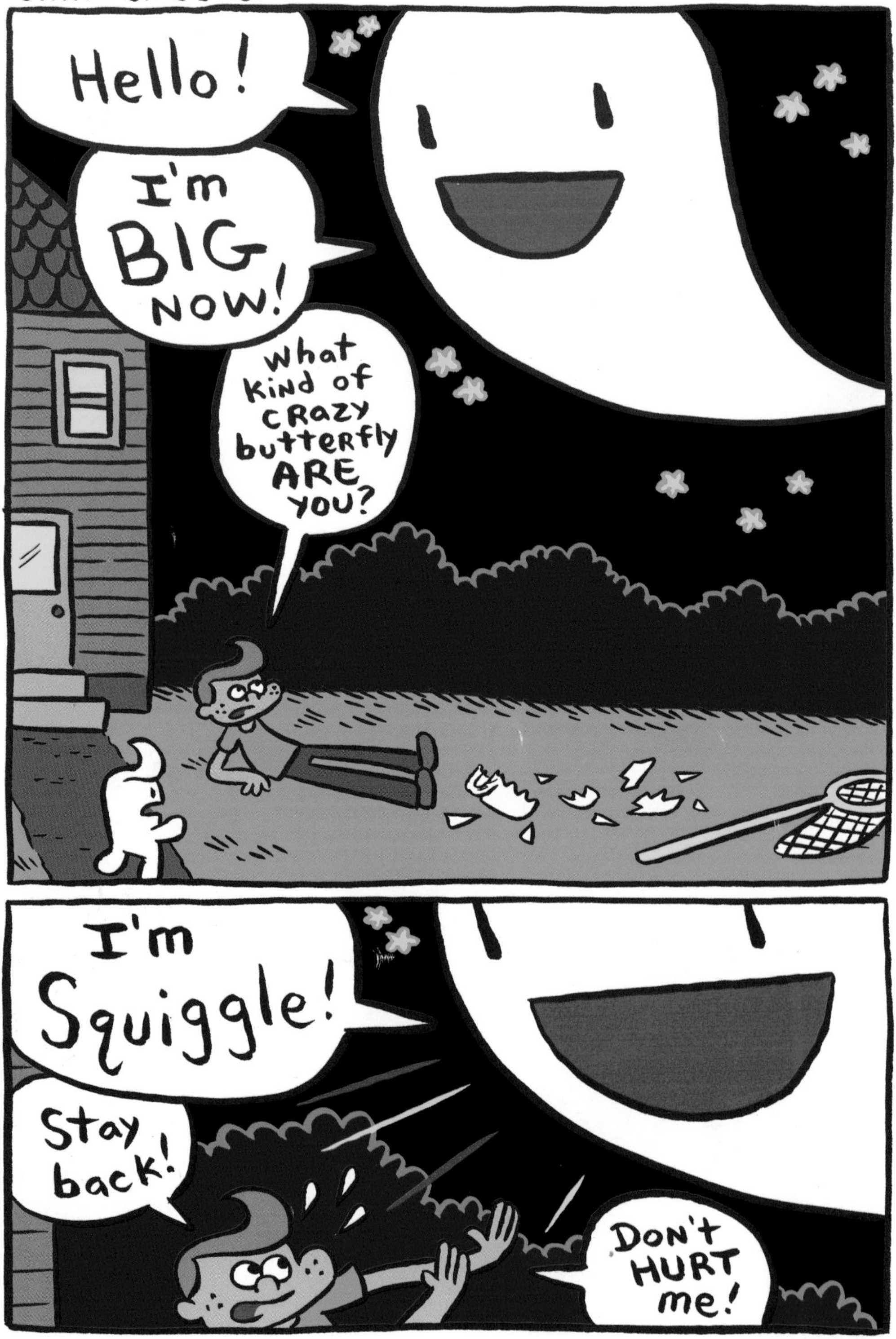
Hello!
I'm BIG NOW!
What kind of CRAZY butterfly ARE YOU?
I'm Squiggle!
Stay back!
DON'T HURT me!

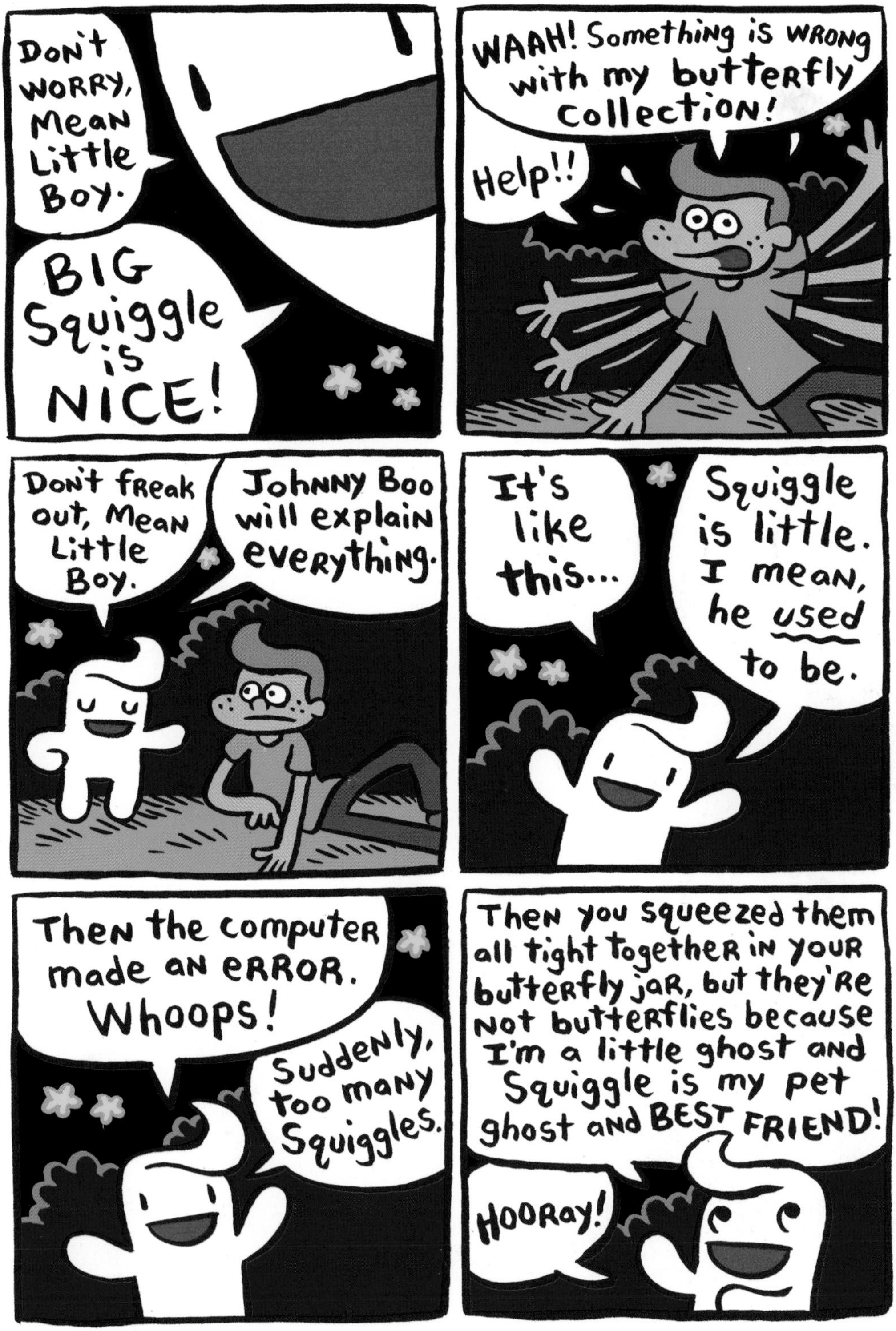
Don't worry, Mean Little Boy.
BIG Squiggle is NICE!
WAAH! Something is wrong with my butterfly collection!
Help!!
Don't freak out, Mean Little Boy.
Johnny Boo will explain everything.
It's like this...
Squiggle is little. I mean, he used to be.
Then the computer made an error. Whoops!
Suddenly, too many Squiggles.
Then you squeezed them all tight together in your butterfly jar, but they're not butterflies because I'm a little ghost and Squiggle is my pet ghost and BEST FRIEND!
HOORAY!

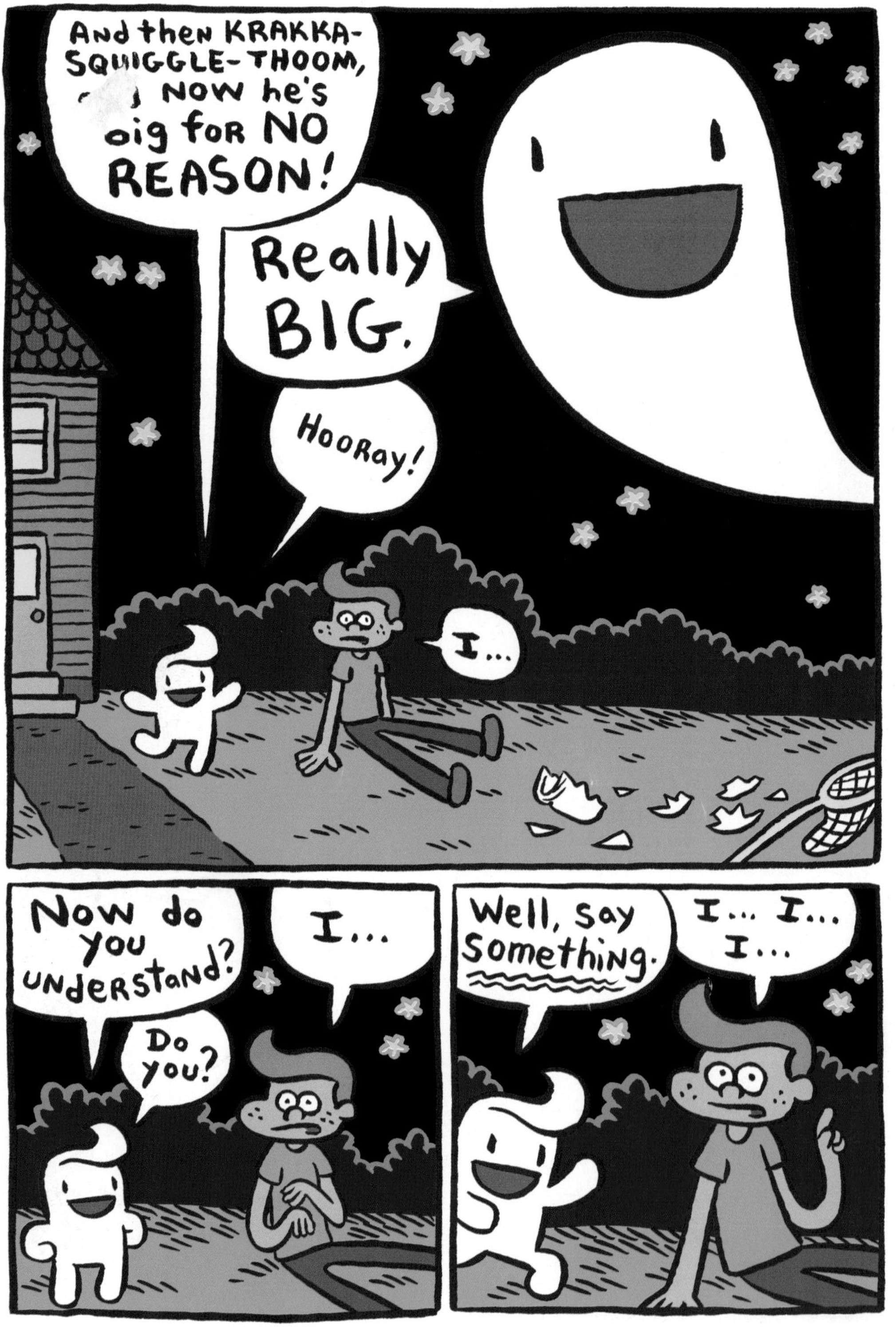
And then KRAKKA-SQUIGGLE-THOOM,
NOW he's big for NO REASON!
Really BIG.
HooRay!
I...
Now do you understand?
Do you?
I...
Well, say Something.
I... I... I...

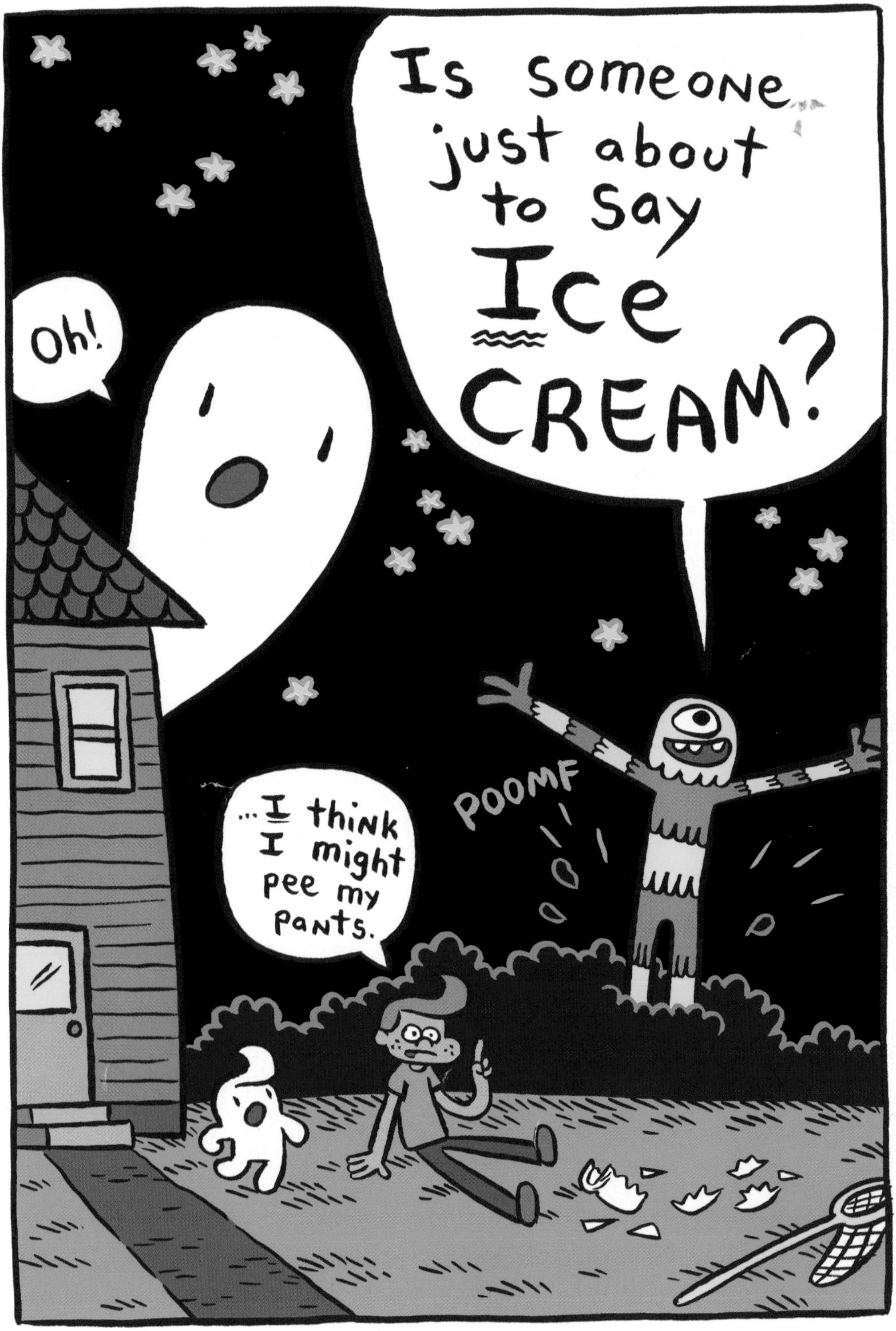
Oh!
Is someone just about to say Ice CREAM?
POOMF
...I think I might pee my pants.

CHAPTER EIGHT

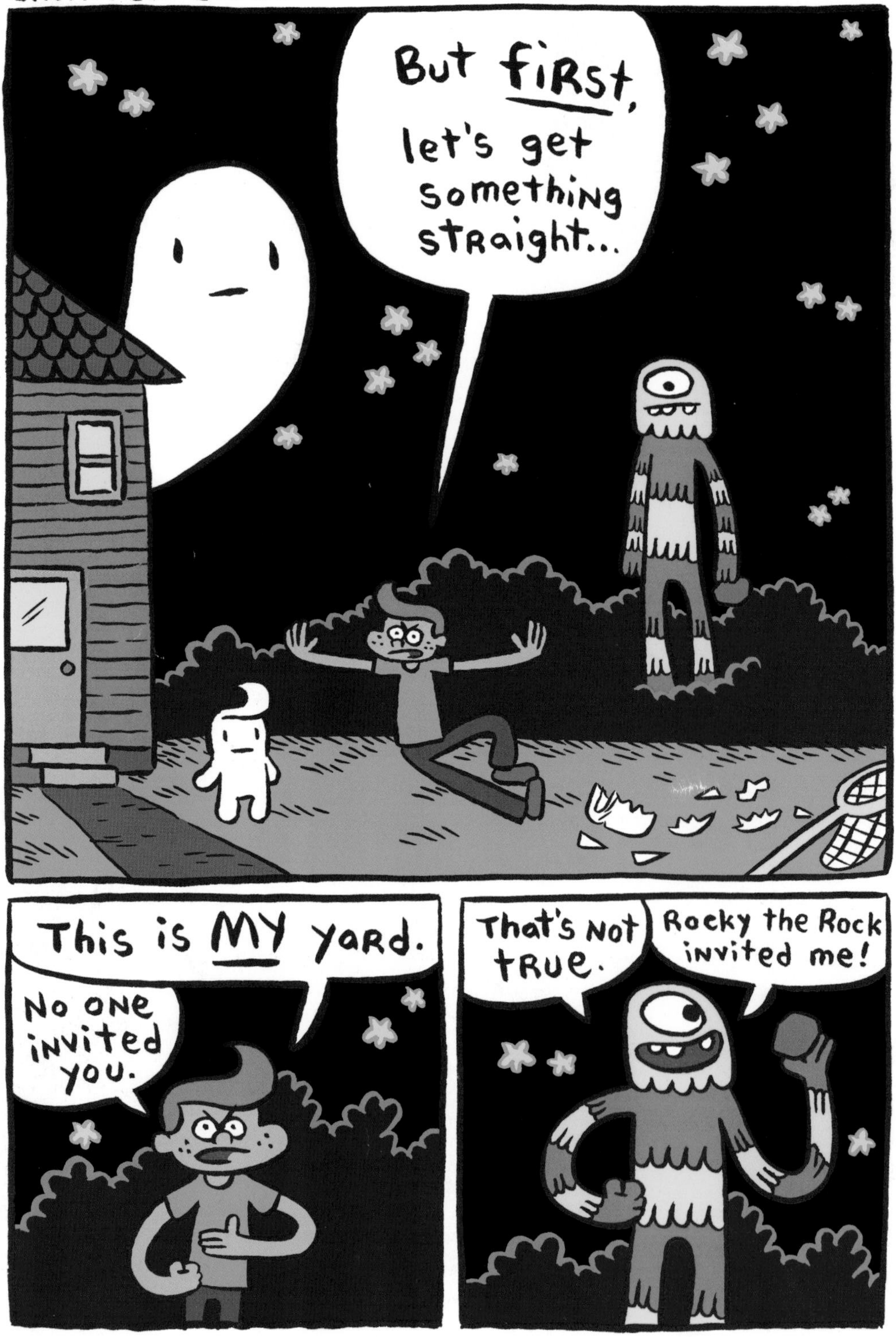

But FIRST, let's get something straight...
This is MY yard.
No one invited you.
That's not true.
Rocky the Rock invited me!

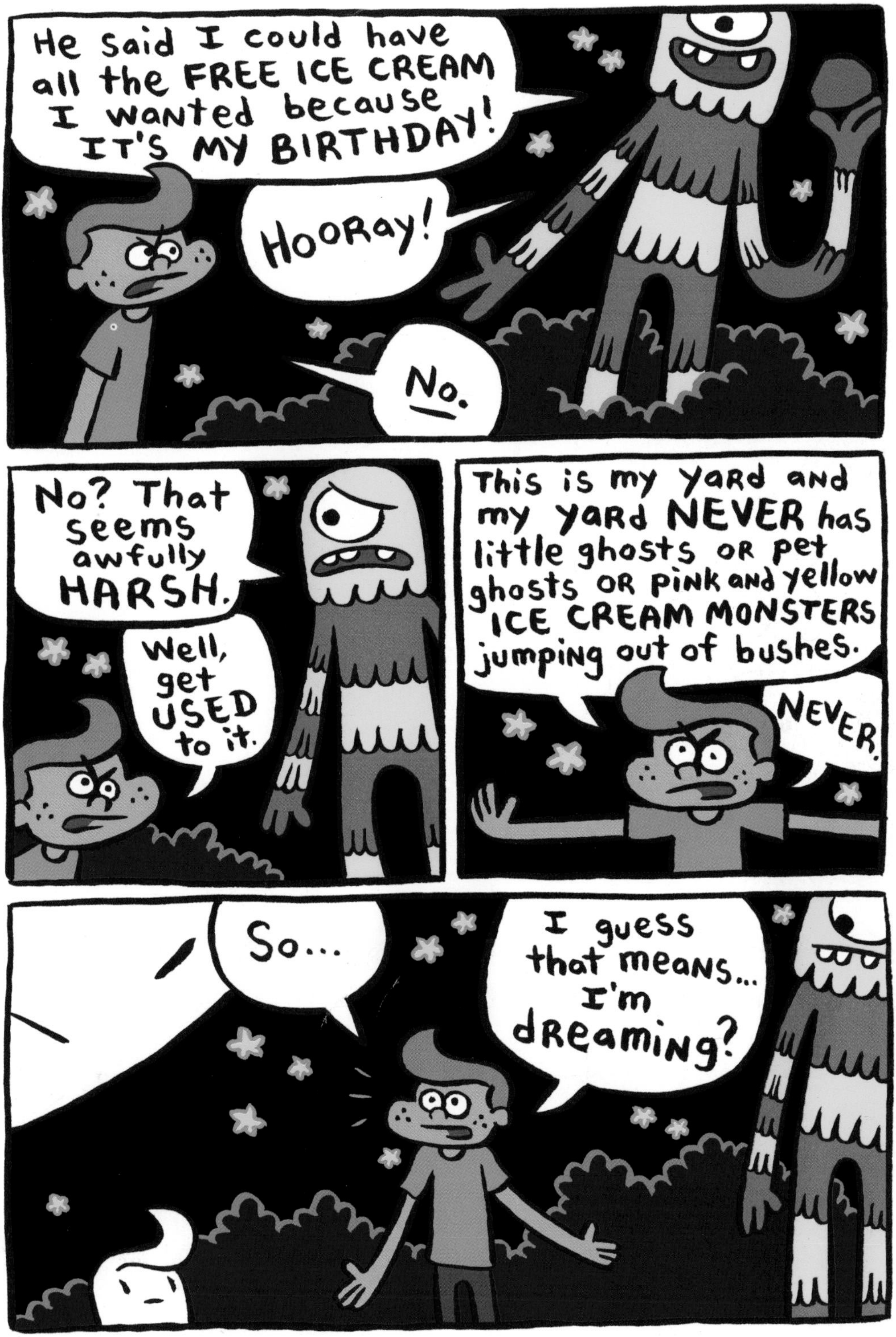
He said I could have all the FREE ICE CREAM I wanted because IT'S MY BIRTHDAY!
HOORAY!
No.
No? That seems awfully HARSH.
Well, get USED to it.
This is my yard and my yard NEVER has little ghosts or pet ghosts or pink and yellow ICE CREAM MONSTERS jumping out of bushes.
NEVER.
So...
I guess that means... I'm dreaming?

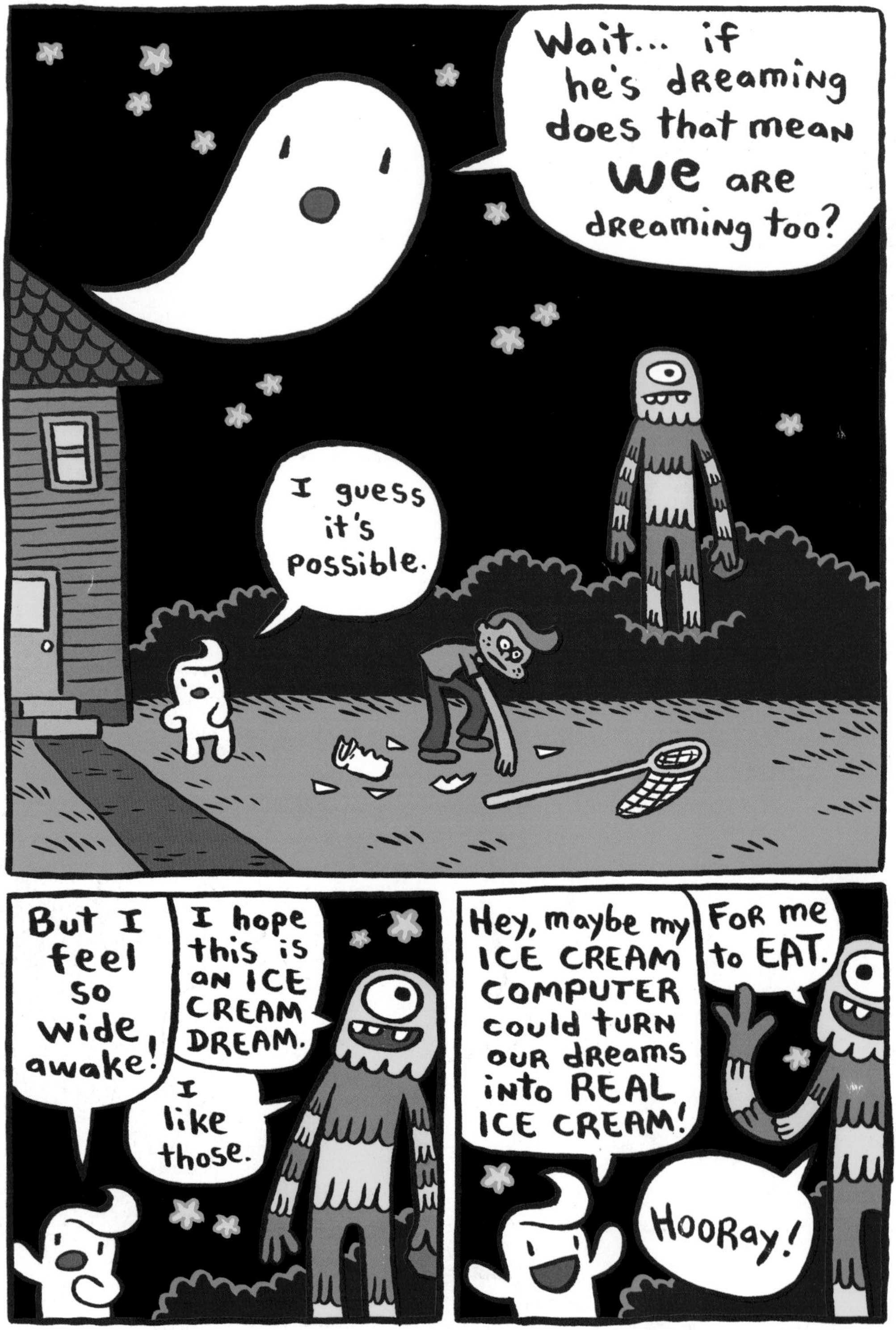
Wait... if he's dreaming does that mean WE are dreaming too?
I guess it's possible.
But I feel so wide awake!
I hope this is an ICE CREAM DREAM.
I like those.
Hey, maybe my ICE CREAM COMPUTER could turn our dreams into REAL ICE CREAM!
For me to EAT.
HOORay!

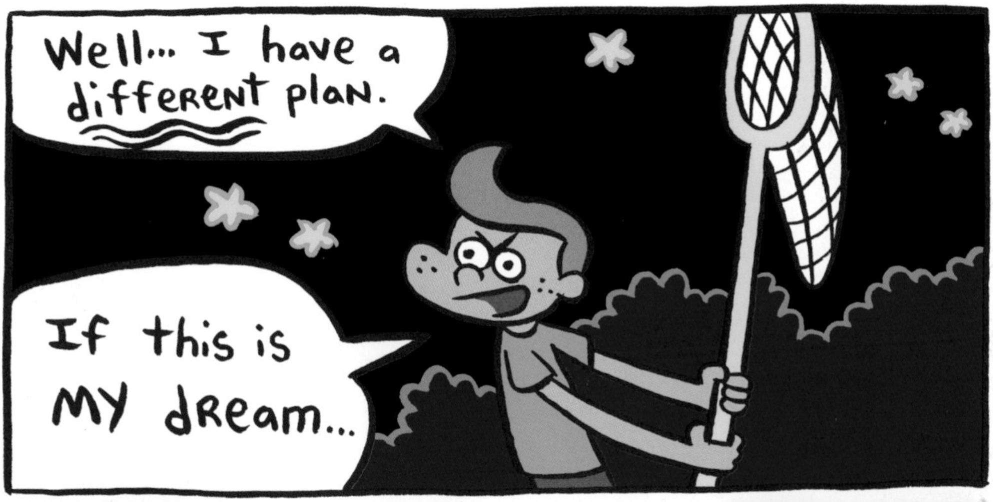
Well... I have a different plan.
If this is my dream...

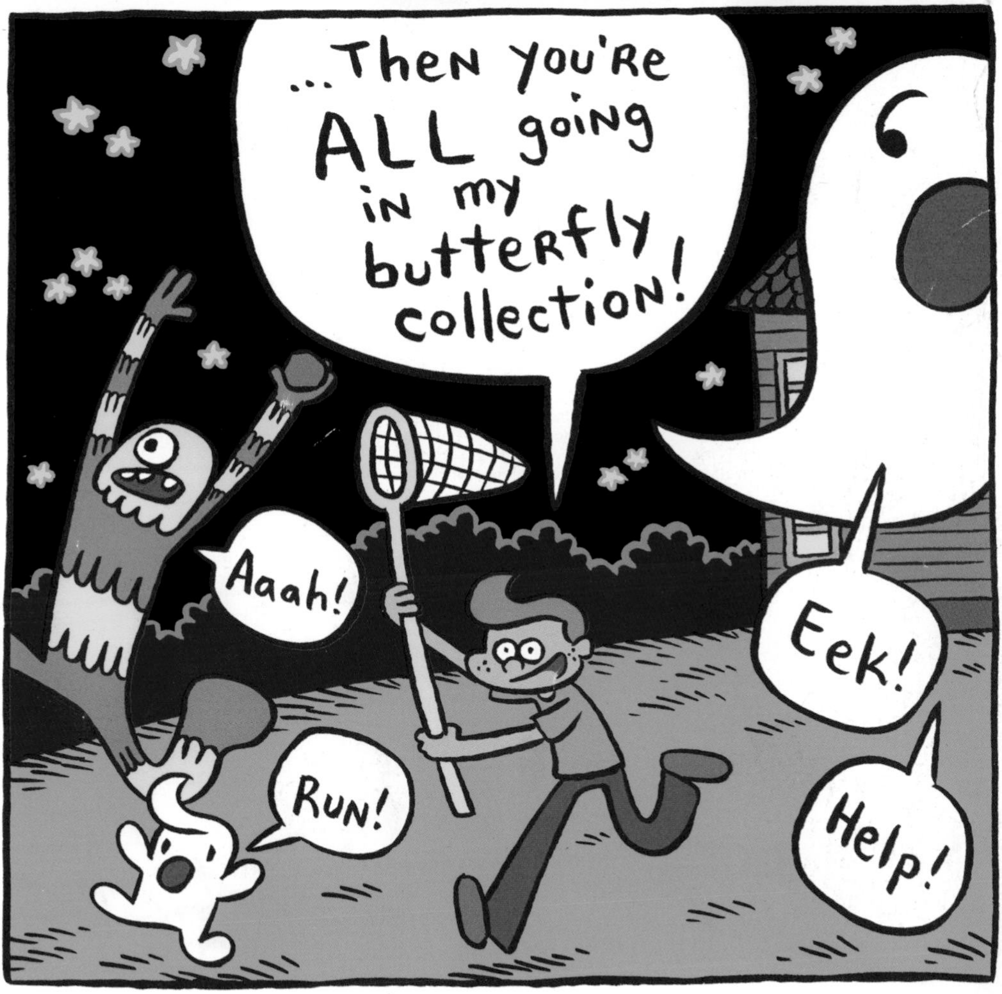
...Then you're ALL going in my butterfly collection!
Aaah!
Run!
Eek!
Help!

CHAPTER NINE

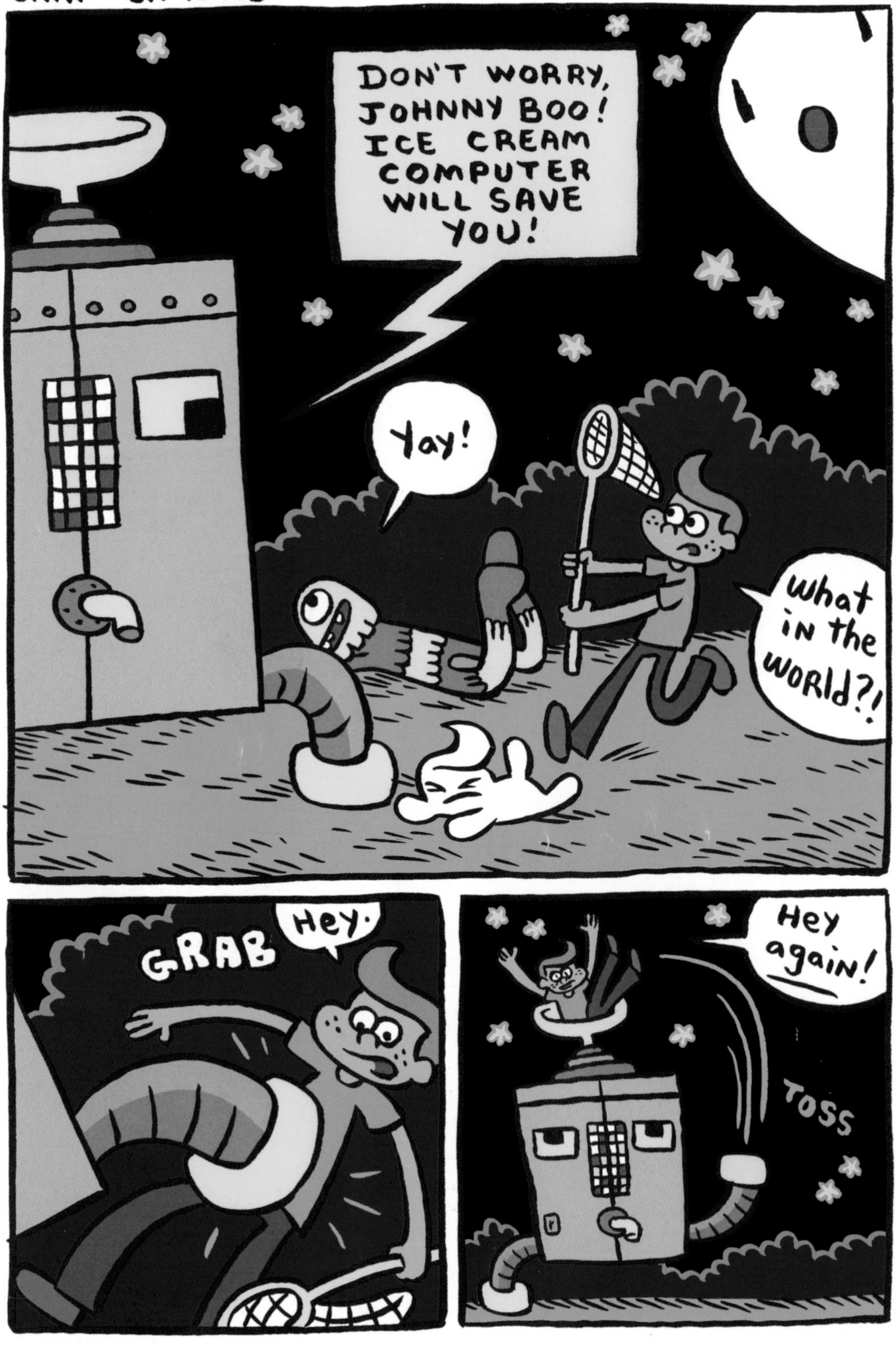
DON'T WORRY, JOHNNY BOO! ICE CREAM COMPUTER WILL SAVE YOU!
Yay!
What in the world?!
GRAB
Hey.
Hey again!
TOSS

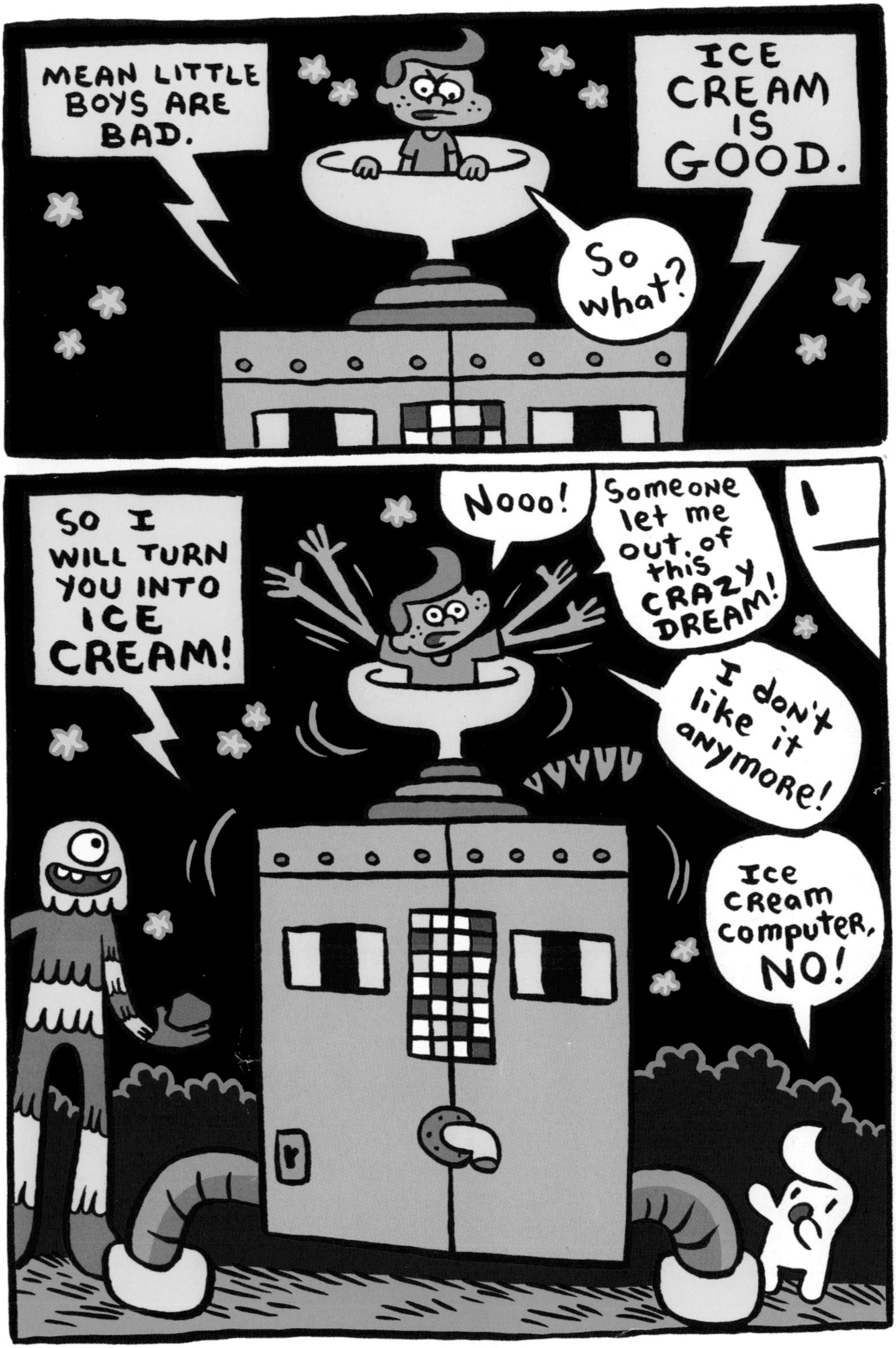
MEAN LITTLE BOYS ARE BAD.
So what?
ICE CREAM IS GOOD.
SO I WILL TURN YOU INTO ICE CREAM!
Nooo!
Someone let me out of this CRAZY DREAM!
I don't like it anymore!
Ice cream computer, NO!

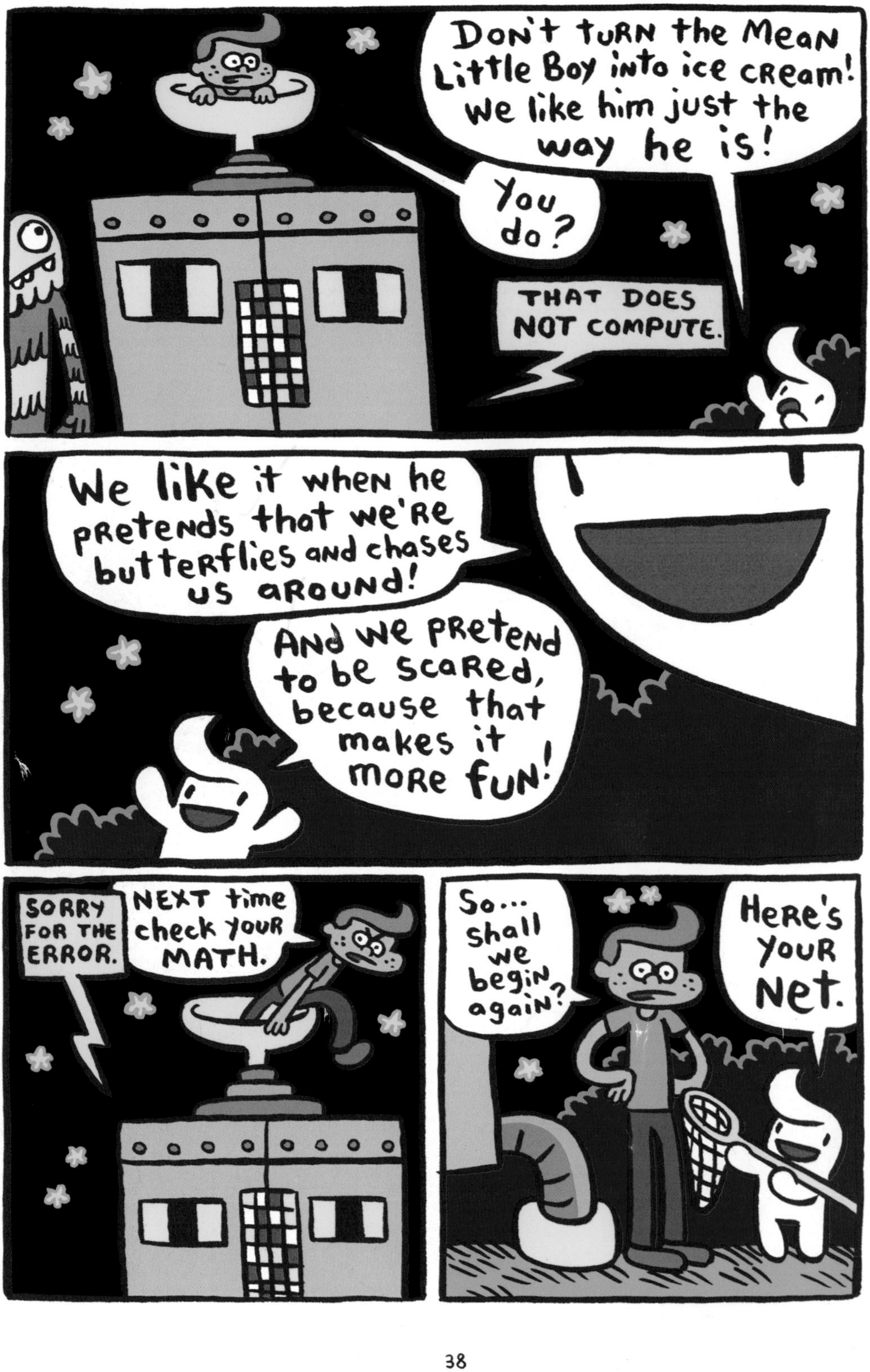
Don't turn the Mean Little Boy into ice cream! We like him just the way he is!
You do?
THAT DOES NOT COMPUTE.
We like it when he pretends that we're butterflies and chases us around!
And we pretend to be scared, because that makes it more fun!
SORRY FOR THE ERROR.
NEXT time check your MATH.
So... shall we begin again?
Here's your Net.

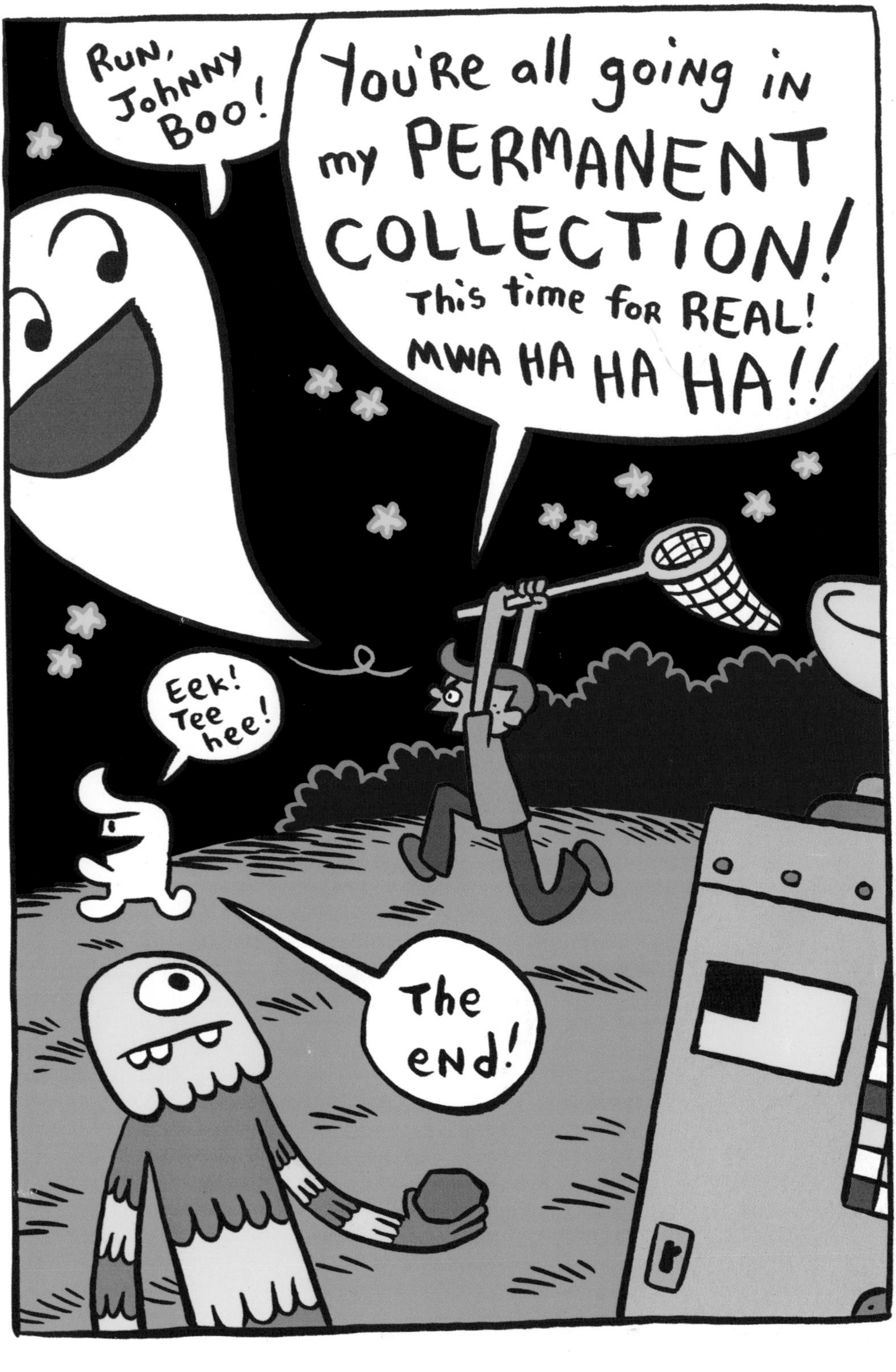
RUN, JOHNNY BOO!
YOU'RE all going IN my PERMANENT COLLECTION! This time FOR REAL! MWA HA HA HA!!
Eek! Tee hee!
The eNd!

CHECK ONE

☑ I THINK THIS STORY
WAS JUST A DREAM.

☑ I THINK THIS STORY
REALLY HAPPENED.

☑ OTHER

PLEASE DISCUSS